USA TODAY BESTSELLING AUTHOR
BRITTNI CHENELLE

For Lydie
An incredibly talented writer, a fierce advocate of
diversity, and a true friend.

 Nova

I stepped to the cliff's edge and peered down into the endless abyss. The sun hadn't yet shown signs of rising, and the last of the stars lingered in the dark like the first snowflakes of the season. A frigid chill passed through me as I instinctively recoiled from the danger. The wind pulled tears from my eyes and mixed them with the morning's cold, blue haze, swirling together with my golden hair, like brush strokes in Van Gogh's Starry Night.

My toes hung over the edge.

The wind's forceful gusts threatened me, thrashing at my back and behind my trembling knees, howling for me to jump. Hedging my courage, I willed myself to glance down once again. I saw nothing but darkness and the silhouettes of the clouds below, dipped in silver-spattered light. I leaned into the open air, yearning for chaos.

I can't live forever.

Just as my body tipped, I stalled for a moment in sweet suspension before I plunged into the darkness.

The contents of my stomach threatened to rise to my throat as the air pounded my skin, closing in around me. It choked my air supply, and I gasped for breath. I relished the twinge of panic that rattled me to the core. It thrilled me. It was my reason why.

I felt death looming, waiting to welcome me like a familiar face, one passed a thousand times. I reached out, acting purely on instinct, grasping for anything to stop my descent, only to feel the kiss of emptiness against my hand as I hurtled out of control, down toward the world below.

The chaos gave way to routine as I angled my body parallel to the Earth, an emergency maneuver all Gardeners had to learn in survival training—the same training I'd completed nine years ago—but this was not an emergency. This was a ritual. A shrill whistle shot through the air below me. My fall halted, and in seconds, I was weightless. My golden hair spilled across my shoulders, and my blood evened out as the soft, leathery wings of my dragon lifted me back up to the world above.

"Good morning, Vex," I whispered with my lips pressed against the soft, shiny scales on his back.

His muscles rippled across his massive body as his iridescent wings flapped against the wind. Each time I rode him, it brought me back to the very first time when he'd chosen me at my Independence Ceremony. Though it had been only nine years, it felt like forever ago. That ceremony had done for me just what my mother had promised. It had turned me from a nine-year-old kid living on an island that felt impossibly small to a dragon-riding adult, free to roam the skies. I had no doubt that the Totem Ceremony tomorrow would change my life just as much. More so, even.

The question was, was I ready?

Vex's body was hardly visible against the gray of the sky. His scales had changed to match the misty morning, but I didn't need to see my dragon well to know I'd summoned the right one. I could tell by his heartbeat. Each dragon's distinctive beat was like a fingerprint. Unmistakable despite their identical forms.

A hint of sunlight slipped through the clouds, reflecting a beam of orange across Vex's silhouette.

I took a deep breath, inhaling the peace and exhaling it into the silence. By midday, the skies would be filled with other riders on the backs of their dragons. I had to make the most of the sky while it was still mine.

Vex rose higher in the sky with each powerful

stroke of his wings and the morning sun followed suit, climbing from the depths, one rich beam of light at a time. I signaled Vex to turn around so I could get a good look at The Garden just as the sun rose. The island hung far above the Earth like a halo. Its greenery spilled over the edges of the landmass along with the rivers and waterfalls that shrouded the bottom of the island in a thick and heavy mist that glowed orange in the sun. I loved the way it shone at this time of day, but after nine years of taking the same flight, The Garden looked different, somehow. I traced my gaze across the lush canopy, pausing on the trees beneath where my home was nestled. I'd lived there for eighteen years, and now I had to say goodbye.

For the last few months, all anyone my age could talk about was our potential placements. We'd seen the ceremony, of course, every year, but this was different. It was finally our turn, and as exciting as that was, there was no denying that our whole future boiled down to this one moment. Tomorrow night I'd be named as a member of one of the four totems, and I'd leave The Garden to protect an element of the Earth.

Would I be named one of The Zoi, guardians of Earth's wildlife, plants, and animals? Or The Atmos, guardians of Earth's oceans, lakes, and rivers? The Gin, guardians of Earth's mountains, deserts, and valleys?

Or would I be lucky enough to land my dream place-ment? The Sylphs, guardians of the wind, sky, and stars.

I wasn't delusional enough to believe I was worthy of such a rare and prestigious placement, but this was my last day to imagine it before that dream died forever. Regardless of where I'd wind up, I'd have to say goodbye to everything I know... *and everyone*. I clenched my jaw at that last thought, not because I had finally started to process everything I'd be giving up for my totem, but because of the face that came to mind first.

PHILANDRO

When I was eleven, I saw a girl leap off the edge of the Garden. I'd been playing with my little brother, Castor, at the edge of the forest when we'd spotted her standing alone by the cliff's edge.

She looked to be around nine years old. Old enough to have a sky dragon, but if she'd had one, she hadn't mounted it.

"She's not going to jump," Castor insisted as he tugged on my arm to bring me back to play.

I watched her silhouette drop. I waited for a sky dragon to land nearby when suddenly she was gone. Without thinking, I sprinted toward the cliffs. My heart pounded in my throat. I whistled for my dragon, but I knew very well that I was far too late. I dropped to my knees at the edge of the cliff, hot tears streaking my face. I reached a hand out to the air as if I expected her to reach back. The wind was knocked out of my lungs, drawing my scream with silence. Before I could find any words, she rose through the clouds on the back of her dragon.

I'd never seen another Gardner attempt to mount their dragon that way. It was too much of a risk. Nor in the nine years of friendship that followed had I ever found the courage to ask her why she had done that. I'd never told her so, but the trauma of that day lingered. Ever so often, I'd dream about it—only for some reason, in the dreams, she never made it.

I trudged through the dewy forest, feeling the chill of the early morning as I made my way to the cliffs, silently cursing Nova for corrupting my morning routine with hers. The day we'd met, the day I'd first seen her jump, she had teased me mercilessly for crying there on the cliff's edge—as unmoved by my concern as Castor.

I whistled for my dragon, Fang. He was waiting at the cliff's edge when I arrived. I mounted him the normal way, like a sane person, and then took off to catch up with Nova. As we flew, I wiped the sleep from my eyes. I definitely didn't consider myself a morning person, but this was the only time I could sneak away.

I didn't see her until after the sun had started to rise. I tightened my grip and kicked my heels into

Fang to increase his speed. The wind sent my hair whipping around my eyes, and I breathed in the morning mist as I closed the gap between Nova and me. Then the moment came, the moment that kept me waking up before dawn, despite my body protesting it every day.

A sense of peace settled in, and Nova looked over her shoulder and grinned. "Lan, you made it! I was so sure you were going to oversleep today."

I had stayed up half the night playing this day over and over in my head. This was my last opportunity to tell her how I felt—the last day before her Totem Ceremony. No matter what, whether the moment presented itself or not, I was going to tell her.

She looked deliriously happy. Her hair tossed about like she'd been struck with lightning.

"Nice hair," I teased.

"Nice face," she said, reigning in Vex.

Fang instinctively slowed, gliding alongside them. I winced, but my chest filled with warmth. I waited to speak in case this was going to be one of those mornings where we flew silently.

"So—" Nova started.

Here we go.

"—How's the courting going? Was it Raven you were supposed to see? I forget."

"Why? You interested in throwing your horse in the race?"

"Meh. Immortality seems overrated."

It was her usual banter, but that never made it sting less. Had we just been friends too long for her to see me any other way? I could feel my confidence slipping through my fingers like water. I was so in my head that I'd only half processed what she said when she spoke again.

"Actually, I told Rose I'd talk her up."

That was a stake to my heart. "Rose?" I asked, scratching the back of my head.

"What do you think of her?"

Ugh. She's not you. "She's perky."

"She's really nice, and I know you think she's pretty."

"Can we talk about... anything else?"

She smirked, and I could see the pleasure she took from my discomfort in the twist of her pursed lips.

"Let's talk about your hair," I said.

"Puh-lease. You think *you're* so cute?"

"No. You're the one who thinks I'm cute." Fang swayed away from Vex and settled back as a breeze pushed between our dragons. I readied myself for her witty retort, but she said nothing. It might have been an illusion from the rising sun, but it almost looked like she was blushing. What was she doing? *This is it. My moment. Say it Lan. Say it.*

"You're not getting weird on me, are you?"

What the fuck was that?

"What? Of course not, you idiot. It's just... with my Totem Ceremony coming up, we might not get a chance to do this anymore."

*Wait a minute...*I tilted my head. *Who is this? Miss independent herself is getting soft?* This was definitely another opening. It might have been fear, but part of me wanted to keep things as light as they'd always been. I'd never forgive myself if I ruined our last day together and our friendship in one stupid, unrequited confession.

I must have been silent for too long because she said, "Sorry. You're right. I'm getting weird. I just don't want things to change between us."

It's now or never.

My heart slammed into my ribs as I said the words. "I do."

"You do what?"

Alarms went off in my head, but it was too late to stop. "I want things to change between us."

Nova

I scanned Lan's honey-colored eyes, waiting for the punchline. His sandy brown curls bobbed in the breeze, with each of his dragon's movements. I swallowed the lump in my throat as the air between us thickened in a way neither of us had ever allowed it to before. Our routine splintered as slices of newness cut through it. Tension, awkwardness, heat. My mind screamed, *What do you mean by that, Lan?* But I couldn't get the words out. Nine years I'd held a candle for him. Nine years I'd been too scared to even jot his name down in my diary for fear he'd find out. It had been nine years since I'd seen the crown prince weeping at the edge of the cliff for me, and he chose the day before my totem ceremony to make such a bold implication.

The last thing I wanted to do was turn to mush around him like everyone else—to hunt him like some sport, not after all the years of him explaining how that behavior made him feel. But he clearly didn't know how irresistible he really was—for me...for everyone. He hadn't needed to grow into his looks like Castor. He was a total Adonis, not to mention sweet, charming, and kind to everyone.

Say something, Nova. Something.

My words kept slamming into the same wall. He'd told me so many times how I was different, but I wasn't. I was exactly the same. I, too, dreamed of eternity alongside him. I just wasn't brave enough to say so like the others. If anything, the other girls were more worthy.

My thoughts took a sudden turn as the negative emotions tipped the scale in their favor. *Maybe he meant something else. Of course, he doesn't have feelings for me—but what else could he mean?*

The silence was laden with tension until the bells of the Garden chimed, filling the air with a pleasant melody that echoed in all directions. Our sky dragons instinctively began heading back to the Garden. Years of muscle memory had trained them well. I said nothing, and asked nothing, even as I felt the moment slipping away.

Vex and Fang landed on the eastern cliffs. Lan and

I dismounted in silence, and I stroked Vex's smooth, iridescent scales before he took to the sky.

I felt the heat of Lan's gaze on my cheek, so I turned to him, desperate to break the silence.

This was just nerves.

He was just sad because I was his best friend, and I'd most likely never see him again after I got my placement.

"I'm going to miss you too," I said, forcing a solemn smile.

I turned away from the cliff, away from Philandro, telling myself to ignore my feelings.

Or was that what I'd been doing all this time?

I felt a warm palm on my arm. I turned to see Lan. His thumb moved slowly across my shoulder, and his gaze was affixed on the ground. It was an innocent gesture, but it set my skin on fire. "Lan," I whispered.

His gaze rose to meet mine. I saw the answers to all my questions in his eyes.

I hadn't imagined it.

Before a fraction of joy slipped in, despair swept it away. Unless I got the Totem I wanted, this would be goodbye forever.

"I know," he said, reading me. "But you could make Sylph. It's what you want anyway, and you'd be close enough. Then maybe we could—"

"Brother—" A voice shot from behind us.

Lan dropped his hand from me as Prince Castor stepped out from the shadows on the forest's edge.

"Oh," he said, his gaze darting between me and Lan.

Damnit, Castor. Why now?

He smirked. "Father is requesting our presence immediately."

Castor brushed his jet-black hair back behind his ear. His grin amplified any awkwardness that might have been floating around. Heat rushed to my face, and I thanked Sol that I could hide the blush beneath my darker complexion.

Castor turned to give us privacy, but there was no need. Any trace of the softness of that moment had been swept away from Lan's eyes, and all that was left was cold, hard focus. He had always been like this. Duty above all. He acted this way whenever his father called, but his lack of hesitation stung a little.

The Crown Prince had better things to do than whatever we had going on. I wasn't sure I'd get another moment alone with him before the ceremony, and the conversation we'd almost had was the one I'd been dreaming about for nine years. I felt the prick of tears as frustration tore through me, and my hatred—

misplaced as it may have been—was directed straight at Castor.

Castor, the second son. Trouble-maker, womanizer, and apparently, blessed by Sol with the worst timing ever.

I watched Lan as he headed into the forest with Castor, but he didn't look back.

PHILANDRO

I cracked my knuckles as Castor and I neared the Garden Palace. The wooden structure rose from the ground like a dense forest, capped with a lush green canopy. The golden accents that bordered the windows and doors tossed errant rays of sun through the forest like glowing fairies at play. It didn't seem to matter to my nerves that my father was a just and fair king. I couldn't shake the stress from my body, nor remember the last time I'd felt so anxious. A request from Father in the middle of the day? What could it be?

Castor grinned, no doubt reveling in my discomfort. It must be nice to be the second son. He seemed to live such a carefree life, never having to worry about duty, free to bask in the privileges of royalty without the expectations. I used to feel sorry for him. It seemed unfair that he would never have his chance to rule, but he'd always assured me that suited him just fine, and only now, as some of the pressure started to press down on me, could I finally understand why.

"Are you alright, brother?"

"Of course." My reply came too quickly to be believed, and Castor's smile only grew.

He raised an eyebrow, and I shoved him playfully. I pushed open the double doors, and my thoughts flipped to Nova. I couldn't help but wonder if some of my nervousness had to do with her. What if my father had called me here to give his permission to marry?

I reeled as I walked through the palace, my thoughts completely consumed with possibilities. We were only friends, but today something new had joined us on our flight. I couldn't let her leave for her placement without investigating it, but none of that meant she'd marry me. She wouldn't possibly give up her Totem for me. Did the fact that I was thinking about it mean I wanted to marry her?

I took a deep breath before I entered the Grand Hall.

"Wait." Castor reached out his arm to block me.

"What?" My voice was cold and shaky.

Castor chuckled. "Take a minute to calm down. Father shouldn't see you this way."

I turned to face him, silently thanking Sol I had a brother.

Castor grinned, pointing to his dimpled cheeks as if I needed a tutorial. His playfulness was endearing, even if it pointed out just how different our lives were. My gaze moved to his dimples, and I grinned. They were the only feature we shared. We do not inherit genes like the humans do. My curly, honey-brown hair and sunny eyes don't resemble Castor's straight, jet black hair and charcoal eyes, and my broad build couldn't have been more different than Castor's slender frame and pointed nose and chin. Even our temperaments differed. Mine being social, dutiful, and composed, and his being standoffish and mischievous. All of this seemed to suggest we weren't brothers at all, but our matching dimples always made me feel more connected somehow.

He stretched his arms over his head and let out a breathy sigh, but it did little to alleviate my nerves.

"So uh... you and Nova, huh?" Castor smirked. "Finally took the plunge."

I cracked my knuckles.

Castor continued, "I've been telling you for years that she's a total fox—"

The doors swung open.

"Boys." My father's voice thundered off the walls

like it was made of something tangible. "You've arrived." He walked over from the center of the hall, his presence heavy and warm in the room. He placed his hand awkwardly on my shoulder and smiled at me and Castor, a toothy grin that we'd rarely seen. "We have much to discuss."

"What is it, Father?" I asked, unable to mask my eagerness.

Castor rolled his eyes.

Father's chest swelled with pride. "Philandro, I've been thinking about this for some time. I'm very proud of the man you've grown into, and I think it's time that you took over the throne."

It was so sudden that I thought I'd imagined it. "Father." I said, but the rest of my words never came.

Castor's hands landed on my shoulders, and he shook me back and forth, his excitement beaming brightly from his face.

The King continued. "Which means it's time for you to select a wife."

"Hah!" Castor blurted. "I think he knows just the one."

Father straightened his posture. "You do?"

I glared at Castor. "No, I don't."

The King's gaze darted between us. "So you don't?"

Castor smirked. "That's not what it looked like."

I fought the urge to punch the smug bastard. The last thing I needed was to have all this broadcasted around The Garden before I even knew how I felt about it. My father eyed me, waiting for a legitimate answer.

My cheeks filled with heat. "I mean, I uh... I might."

Castor shrieked with excitement, "Well, obviously, this is a very important decision. You have an eternity at stake, but I trust your judgment. When you've made your selection, we'll begin preparations. Now, you'll have to excuse me. There's much I need to prepare for the upcoming Totem Ceremony."

Stunned and bewildered, Castor yanked me toward the door. He was practically skipping, but my thoughts were a jumbled mess, and my whole life shaken by the bomb my father had dropped on me so casually.

"Not so fast, Castor," The King said.

Castor froze.

"I need to speak with you alone." My father turned back to me. "I will come find you later to discuss this transition, but right now, I have important business with your brother. You are dismissed."

Important business with Castor? I found it diffi-cult to move. I gazed at my brother, who now seemed as nervous as I'd been earlier. Castor's dark eyes pleaded with me to stay, and I wanted nothing more than to oblige, but that was a direct order.

One I couldn't disobey.

I had no choice, and Castor knew it, but I was sure wherever my father had to say couldn't be as life-altering as the news he dropped on me.

Whatever it was, Castor would no doubt give me an earful when I saw him later, so I forced myself to leave him. But, by Sol, if I had known what was about to befall him, I would have sooner disobeyed the King than not have stood by his side while everything he loved was torn away.

NOVA

I returned to my woodlot home with a new sense of life, my mind replaying my last conversation with Lan.

"Mother?" I called, but there was no reply.

I was grateful for it. I had too much on my mind to sort out without adding in other people's questions. For years I'd listened to the other girls in the Garden fantasize about winning Prince Philandro's immortal heart. They'd interrogated me relentlessly about my frequent meetings with him and pleaded with me to take them along. I'd routinely told them that he was just a friend and that I didn't feel anything more for him, but that hadn't been true for some time.

I don't know exactly when it changed, but Lan had become a part of my day that I couldn't imagine losing, as precious to me as my morning flight on the back of Vex. *I can't believe it*, I mused. *He likes me too.* I walked through my home aimlessly, picking up one chore only to set it down and start another. With my anxiety so on edge, I didn't have the focus to do anything. *I have to make Sylph tomorrow.*

Getting assigned to a position on the earth would ruin everything. No doubt he'd find someone to replace me. Every girl in the Garden was after him for one reason or another. My whole life was riding on the Totem Ceremony. I sank into a chair beside my kitchen table.

I heard a shrill yell. I spun and saw Rose burst through the door. "Did you hear the news? Prince Philandro's getting married!"

I stood, emotionally whiplashed. "What? To who?"

"No one knows, but apparently, the king is going to make him choose someone!"

My face flared with heat.

"I think I have a real shot. Last week I said 'What's up' to him, and he smiled. We totally had a moment." Rose's hands flailed as she excitedly recounted every interaction she had with the prince, but I hardly even noticed.

My thoughts were consumed with questions, crashing over each other like waves. I had to see Lan before tomorrow, before the Garden decided my fate,

Rose's, and that of all the rest of the 17-year-old Gardeners.

"Rose I—"

"And just last week," she went on, "he didn't say hi, but we had some very meaningful eye contact."

It was a mess. We hadn't even figured out what we meant to each other, and now marriage was on the table? Was there some kind of timetable? Was I even being considered?

"Rose, I think..." I stopped.

Rose was so lost in her own story that I couldn't get a word in edgewise, and the more she talked, the more anxious I felt.

I need to talk to Lan. Now. Without thinking, I rushed out of my home, leaving Rose in the kitchen without a word.

I raced back into the forest, and the sounds of Rose, in my kitchen, going through all the girls she thought she was competition with, faded into the distance.

I wove through the trees, dashing over the Garden's lush, green terrain, which teemed with life, leaping over ascending roots that got in my way. The morning was shrouded in a thick mist that made the path difficult to see and the stones slippery, but I didn't stop to catch my breath until I made it to the edge of the Garden. My heart nearly burst from my chest when I saw a dark figure in the hazy fog standing at the cliff's edge. *He's here. He came to meet me!*

I took a second to pause and catch my breath, sweeping my hair back into a ponytail. By the time I moved closer, and the grassy terrain underfoot turned rocky, I knew it wasn't Lan. Disappointment filled my mouth with bitterness. *Who else would be out here?* I preferred this spot for the steepness, which was perfect for leaping, but the other Gardeners who flew always mounted on the West side of the Garden.

"Hey," I called. "What are you doing out here?"

The figure thrust himself off the edge. I froze. *What the hell?*

I jogged to the edge, trying to stay calm, listening for the wispy woosh of a dragon's wings. But I heard nothing. I bit down on my bottom lip and glanced around to see if anyone else was nearby, but I was alone. *It has been several years since the last suicide. But maybe the pressure of the Totem Ceremony...*

Feeling the urgency of every second that slipped by, I dove headfirst off the edge.

I kept myself in a perfect line to increase my speed. I knew I'd have to change my angle for Vex to come to my aid, but I needed to catch up to the falling figure first.

I couldn't see him through the gusting wind and scattered cloud cover.

I steadied my nerve as I plummeted faster and farther than I'd ever gone before. Doubt crept into my head. *It's no use. He's gone.* I prepared to signal Ve, but before I could call him, I broke through a line of clouds, revealing the vibrant green earth below. I gasped. Its mass alone was beyond anything that I'd previously imagined. It glittered in blue-green spectra and buzzed with energy, and refracted light.

A few yards below me, I saw the figure hurling toward the earth with no visible indication they were calling for a dragon. Even with his hair wind-tossed and covering his eyes, I knew who it was. *Prince Castor. But why?*

CASTOR

I let my limbs go limp like a ragdoll as I dropped from the sky. I liked the feeling, the illusion of danger. Every year the Totem Ceremony came and went, and directly following it was what I'd carelessly referred to as suicide season. The concept itself seemed childish. When one didn't get placed in the Totem they wanted, they no longer wanted to live? I'd once considered it pathetic. How Sol had made me eat those thoughts. I would never have a Totem Ceremony, but I was damned just the same, and my father dropped the news on me like he'd expected me to be grateful. The worst bit was that, as an immortal, I was robbed of the option to die.

I could at least test the limit of my immortality.

The earth rushed toward me, the blotches of color defining as I neared it. I dropped dangerously low before I heard a dragon screech in my vicinity.

Before I could angle myself to see what the hell was happening, someone's arms wrapped around me from behind.

I was forced to flatten my position, slightly slowing my descent. I fought to break free from their tight grip as homes and trees drew near, and the pine-ridden smell of forest filled my nose.

A dragon swooped into position below me, but we'd picked up too much speed, and the ground was approaching too quickly. The iridescent beast let out a shrill cry as the three of us narrowly missed the steeple of a church, crashing into a forest.

The dragon had taken the brunt of the fall, so I scrambled to my feet, trying to make sense of what the hell had just happened.

A few yards away, I saw a girl sprawled in a mess of splintered wood.

I peered over her, recognizing her immediately. Lan's little friend. *What the hell is she doing here?*

She sat up, tossing her blonde hair over her shoulder and checking herself for injuries.

"What was that?" I asked, malice dripping from my voice. I knew immediately that the anger was a little misplaced.

"Y—you were falling," she stammered as she shied away from me.

"I'm immortal," I said flatly.

Nova's dragon nudged her, prompting her to stand up. Nova started to check him, running her hands along his shimmery back.

Finally, as if I was an afterthought, she said, "What were you doing? I thought you were in trouble."

I clapped slowly, "And what a rescue attempt it was."

Nova sighed, "Sorry."

I scoffed. "That's it? You literally tackle me down to earth, and all I get is 'sorry'?"

"I was speaking to my dragon." She turned to face me. "But I'm sorry I tried to save you. I actually didn't know it was you until just before I grabbed you."

"Isn't this how you tricked my brother?"

Nova smiled, "Actually, he tried to rescue me."

"Oh."

The church hummed with voices in song, and I was grateful that we hadn't accidentally destroyed it.

Nova scanned the thickly wooded forest. "I see why you wanted to come down here. It's very different."

"First time?"

She nodded. "You?"

I shook my head.

Nova squinted in the sun. "It's hot here."

"Could be worse," I mumbled.

We sat in silence until the church bells rang and people started filing out. Nova shifted nervously as even though we were a few paces into the forest, we were in plain view.

"They can't see us, right?" She eyed the humans.

"Nope."

Crowds of people disbursed into the square, away from the forest, but a group of boys in their late teens sat on a stone wall that separated the church from the woods.

Nova watched with fascination, and I had to admit, I'd spent almost no time observing mortals this closely.

"Come on!" One of the boys called to the group from across the square.

Most of the boys hurried over to meet him, but one remained seated on the wall, staring out at the woods, near where we watched. He had messy brown hair and a resigned calm about him that I liked.

"Connor! Let's go!" someone yelled.

The boy called back over his shoulder, "I'll catch up with you later."

The boy's gaze moved back to Nova, and I straightened, following his eye line to see what was drawing his attention. *He couldn't see her, right?*

Nova froze like a deer in headlights. The boy waved

to her, and she turned to me with widened eyes, utter panic dripping from her features.

The boy turned to me, smiled, and then put his hands up as if to say, 'My bad, I didn't mean to scam on your girl.' He promptly hopped off the wall and followed his friends into the square.

"That was weird," Nova said. "It really seemed like that boy could see us."

"Don't be stupid," I said quickly.

It was impossible, and yet, he'd given every indication that he could.

NOVA

I cataloged the differences between the earth's forest and the one in The Garden. There were dead things here. Broken branches, wilted plants. The bark was uneven. Some trees had fallen down and split. It was imperfect, something that I never knew a forest could be.

And even though he had been gone for some time, I couldn't get that boy out of my head. I didn't care what Castor said. That boy had looked right at me.

"Does it seem brighter here?" Castor asked.

I smiled. "Maybe a bit."

Castor nodded. "Strange."

"Prince Castor, do you do this a lot? Come to earth, I mean."

Castor shook his head, and I was sure that was as much as I was going to get from him, but he surprised me.

"Today, I guess, I needed to just get away."

What could a pampered, carefree person like him possibly need to get away from?

"What happened?"

He took a deep breath before answering. "Let's just say my father gave me a gift that feels like a punishment."

What does that mean? I couldn't shake the feeling that it would be impertinent to ask. I'd probably already pried too much. I hopped up from the stump I'd been resting on. "We should go back. I have to prepare for the ceremony tomorrow."

"That's right. You're eighteen this year." For the first time since we'd fallen, Castor smiled. He took a seat on a fallen tree trunk. "Well," he said, "let's see it."

I looked around the empty forest. It chirped and buzzed with presence but appeared to be completely empty, as was the square outside the church.

"Here?"

"Well if you want to impress Lan tomorrow and make Sylph, you'll need constructive criticism."

It couldn't hurt to get someone's opinion other than my mom and Rose. He'd seen a lot of these ceremonies. Maybe my rescue efforts wouldn't be a bust after all.

I took my first position, and my hands crossed at the wrists above my head. "Don't laugh."

"I wouldn't dream of it."

I brought my arms down and spun. Next, I spread my arms, lunged to the right, and stepped back, continuing each meticulously planned step.

Castor watched with amusement for a moment, then reached into his breast pocket and pulled out a wood-whittled flute. He began to play, matching my rhythm. Slowly, he decreased the speed. I turned to him, confused, keeping in step. He nodded to me, so I slowed my rhythm, matching the melodic tune. We moved like a snake charmer and a viper.

It was still my routine, but it felt different. More like me. My movements grew slower and deeper until Castor's song ended on a high, wavering note.

"Heh, not bad," he said.

"That was better, thanks. I would never have thought of slowing it down. Do you think I'll make Sylph?"

"Nah."

"What?"

"I mean... you nearly killed your dragon today."

"I was trying to save you!"

Castor chuckled as he climbed onto my dragon. He reached his hand out to help me up.

"Let's get you back home. I hear you have some things to discuss with my brother."

I felt myself blush. So Rose's story was, in some part, true. Vex took off, and in no time, was soaring through the air, lifting Castor and I back to the Garden with evenly spaced flaps of his massive wings.

The sun was setting as my dragon descended back on the cliffs. Philandro was sitting at the edge, but jumped up to greet me when he saw my dragon land. Out of the corner of my eye, I saw him recoil for a fraction of a moment when Castor helped me down.

Castor turned to him with a wide grin. "Brother, you're just the person we were looking for."

He patted Philandro playfully on the back and headed back into the forest.

The tension released from Lan's shoulders as I approached with slow, calculated steps. I was no longer sure what I was walking toward. A friend? Something more? My future?

Lan smiled down at me, and his marblesque skin shone in the setting sun.

I wasn't used to him looking at me this way, like I was new. I chuckled at my own fear.

"Interesting day?"

I nodded. "You could say that."

I pulled a thick strand of my golden hair out of my

face and tucked it behind my ear. I wasn't sure how to explain Castor's part in it, so I simplified it as much as I could.

"I uhhh... lost control of my dragon and ended up on the earth below. I kinda ran into your brother there."

Lan's smile lit up his whole face. "Aha! I knew cliff jumping was going to get you into trouble one day."

I laughed.

We fell into a silence that was neither awkward nor comfortable. The air between us buzzed with heat and intensity. I gazed at Lan's handsome face. I'd always admired his sense of justice and the goodness that came so easily to him. But as I looked at him now, I began to have new thoughts. What would it be like to touch him? What would it feel like to be wrapped up in his arms? I wondered if the feeling in the pit of my stomach would subside if I went for it, like a quenched thirst after a long drink of water. Or would it intensify like a match thrown into a blazing fire?

Lan broke the silence between us suddenly, his voice low and musical, "My father asked me to choose a wife."

My heart thudded, my cheeks filled with color.

He continued, "I know we're not ready to even talk about this, even if you didn't have the Totem Ceremony tomorrow. I know that if you don't make Sylph, we'll have to wait ten years to find out what this is..."

He reached into his pocket and pulled out a meticulously carved wooden ring. My body tensed. I pushed out the voice in my head that was screaming 'yes' in order to record every detail of the moment. How I felt standing at the cliff's edge at sunset, in front of Lan, my oldest friend, picturing the rest of my life with him. I had no words for him, but I didn't need them.

He continued without them. "I couldn't let you get your Totem without telling you that it's always been you. It will always be you. No matter what placement you get, I'll wait for you."

Lan slipped the ring on my finger. I forced my hands to stop shaking.

"This is a promise that when you're ready, I'll make you immortal."

I had no words of reply. Nothing. Anything I could have possibly said would have ruined it. Nothing could compare. I stared at the ring on my finger. This might've been building over the years, but it still felt so sudden.

I wanted to give him something in return. Mustering all of my courage, I lifted my chin and leaned into Lan, brushing my lips on his. He wrapped his arm around me and pulled me tight to him. For a moment, it frightened me. Then the soft caress of his lips put me at ease. It was just as I'd always imagined my first kiss, drenched in orange light beside my favorite cliff. It was a new world, one that I felt lucky to be a part of. And just as quickly as it had come, the moment passed in a blur of mixed emotions.

Lan held me as the sun set, and just before we parted ways, he kissed my hand. I knew I'd be too nervous about the ceremony to sleep, but I wished I could. Maybe then I could relive my evening with Philandro, over and over, just in case it was our last.

PHILANDRO

I t was hard to breathe knowing that Nova felt
the same way about me. It was more than I'd
allowed myself to feel since I'd met her, but ever
since that line was crossed, it was all I could think
about. Her lips. The way the sunset lit her face. They
made adrenaline course through my body. I headed
back to the palace with renewed energy for the task I
was about to undertake. Taking the throne didn't seem
so much of a burden if Nova would be ruling beside
me. Change was good. Just yesterday, Nova and I had
been only friends, and today we were on a whole new
trajectory.

I searched the palace for Castor, but I couldn't find
him. He would be the most excited by the news, so
naturally, he was the one I wanted to tell the most. He
wasn't in his room, the library, or the atrium, so he had
to be out. If I thought about it, I hadn't seen much of

him since Father had told me I'd be King, and I had to wonder if he'd changed his position about not wanting the throne. I didn't have long to wait, though. Dinner was in an hour, and it was unlikely that he'd skip one of those.

Sure enough, when I arrived in the dining room, he was already seated at the table in his usual spot. I wasn't sure when I'd last had a good look at him, but something was off. His eyes were sunken, with distinctive dark circles around them. His expression drooped in solemnity, and it took several seconds for him to even look up from his empty plate and notice me standing there. When he finally did, he grinned, but the warmth of it didn't reach his eyes.

I took a seat beside him, but before I could tell him about Nova, the two footmen at the entrance reached out, and each grabbed one of the double doors, pulling them open. My mother strode in, her presence forcing both Castor and me to stand... Only Castor didn't stand. He sat with his head down, even as my mother stood at her seat beside the head of the table.

She'd never been an affectionate or nurturing woman. When Castor and I were younger, my father had said it was because she'd given all of her love to the Totem spirits. She must be feeling remarkably pious today because the icy glare that she gave Castor was so sharp it could have stopped his heart, had he been looking.

I nudged him, and he groaned before begrudgingly standing. My father was next to enter. He was pink-cheeked, and his mood jovial.

"Ah, my sons," he said as he took his place at the head of the table and gestured for the rest of us to sit.

He clapped his hands, and a parade of servants carried in oak platters filled with an orange-colored curry that made my mouth water.

The silence in the room seemed to hinge on the wide range of moods our royal family displayed at the table. I wondered if Castor had gotten into some kind of argument with our mother, which wouldn't have been out of character.

Eager to break the tension, I cleared my throat, but my father beat me to the punch. "So, Philandro, my boy, have you given any more thought to what we spoke of earlier?"

I wasn't sure exactly how much I was ready to divulge, but I wanted him to know I was serious. "I have, Father."

Castor elbowed me.

Father's bushy white eyebrow rose in response to the gesture. "What is it, Castor?"

Castor grinned but kept his gaze on his plate as he

pushed the curry around with his fork. "Lan has a girlfriend."

I couldn't stop the smile from stretching across my face, and I saw my enthusiasm mirrored in my father's face. Even the corners of my mother's mouth turned up a bit.

"Who is it? Do tell us, son," the King said as he downed a large bite of curry.

"Nova."

My father beamed. "Excellent choice, son, excellent."

A wave of relief rushed through me, stopped abruptly by my mother's cold gaze.

"No," she said. "She's not an appropriate choice."

The rest of us stared at her in alarm. My father reached out to her. "My dear—"

"No. She's not an acceptable choice." Her frigid stare landed on my father, and I watched his immortal light wilt under it.

I was too stunned to speak, frozen as my worst nightmare played out in front of me.

"What's wrong with Nova?" Castor asked, "He loves her. That's all that matters."

"You stay out of this." Mother hissed.

The Queen folded her hands together and straightened her posture. "I will compile a list of suitable women who I believe will make an excellent Queen, and when you have come to your senses, you can select one to be your bride."

"That sounds very reasonable," said Father apologetically.

"Like hell it is!" Castor slammed his hand on the table, rattling the dishes.

"Castor!" I had finally found my voice.

"No! Why aren't you more upset about this?" he yelled.

"I-I am. I just—"

"He just knows his place," Mother finished.

I was every bit as angry as Castor, but I had duties that wouldn't be upheld if I flew off the handle every time I disagreed. I'd find another way to convince our parents that Nova was the ideal choice. It was fine. Once she made Sylph, I was certain they'd see how rare and special she was.

Castor scoffed and muttered "Coward," before he stormed out of the dining room.

Father stood.

"Let him go." Mother said.

I knew Castor was just defending me, and I loved him for it, but that didn't mean I had to do things his way. So my mother didn't approve of Nova... it was a solvable problem. It put a little more pressure on the

Totem Ceremony, but I had every faith that she'd become a Sylph.

Looking back, all the signs were there that everyone else at that table had known something I didn't.

NOVA

lacement day broke with a dawn that I didn't view from the back of my dragon. I couldn't remember the last time I'd skipped a morning flight. I'd often taken my chances with bad weather. But today, I lay as still as The Garden statues that watched over us, rehearsing my steps in my mind. I made sure to visualize it with Prince Castor's suggestions, slower and deeper, allowing myself to connect with it fully.

From my bed, I watched my white ball gown, which was dangling, hung on my door, glittering with crystals set ablaze by the morning sun. It was a blank slate, white. Like all the other placement candidates' clothing. But by the ceremony's end, that would change, and I'd be damned if I didn't end my dance wearing the silvery gray of the Sylph Totem. I wondered how the rest of the participants were doing. Had they spent the night as restlessly as I had?

In just a few hours, my fate would be decided, but at least I didn't have to worry about what would happen with Lan. I lifted my hand and looked at the wooden ring he'd placed there. I'd been extremely careful to hide it from my mother after I'd returned home, but had allowed myself to wear it once I'd made it to my room, away from prying eyes. My mother meant well, of course. She'd always hinted that I should make more of my time alone with Lan. What mother wouldn't want her daughter to be immortal? But I just wanted to hold onto the perfect memory a little longer, if I could, before it became fodder for the other Gardeners to devour.

I used to love watching the men and women dance in the ceremony as a child. The magic of the divine decision process was a wonder to anyone who observed, but now that it was my turn, the fear of it eclipsed the glamour. I shivered to think that it could go wrong and I could end up back on the earth below.

Not everyone shared that sentiment. Rose had always dreamed of becoming an Atmos, to serve her years protecting earth's vast oceans. I could see the appeal. From what I'd seen, earth's oceans were far greater than any body of water in the Garden. I was certain that by the midpoint of her dance, I'd see Rose's gown turn blue.

"Bitch!"

I smiled to myself as Rose's voice shot through the window.

"I know you didn't walk out on me yesterday and then not come to tell me why."

I leaped out of bed and poked my head out the window. I waved her up, and she obliged, bounding up the steps so noisily I was sure she'd wake my mother. When she burst into my room, she had her dress slung over her arm, but it was in some kind of bag, so I couldn't get a peek at it. I was supremely curious. Rose was nothing else if not an oversharer, but she'd insisted on keeping the details of her dress hush-hush.

I reached for it.

"Girl, we ain't even friends right now. Where the hell did you go yesterday?"

I took a deep breath through my nose. "You can't tell anyone."

Her eyes got big, and she said, "Hold up." She rushed over to my bed, where she tossed her dress and sat down, legs crossed and fingers interlocked over her knee. "Spill the tea."

I closed my eyes and lifted my hand to show her the ring.

"Noooooooooo!" she gasped, leaping to her feet. "I hate you! Lan proposed?" She ripped the ring off my finger and put it on, then lay across the bed as she admired. "Shiiit, I would have left too."

I laughed as I watched her, and she rolled over to her stomach and glared at me. "If you don't sit the hell down and tell me every single detail, by Sol, I'm going to punch you in the face."

I grinned, taking a seat beside her. "Okay so, we were on our usual morning flight—"

With a knock at my door, my mother peeked in. "I thought I heard Rose. Happy Totem ceremony day, girls!"

"Good morning," Rose said cheerfully.

I shot Rose the eye so that she knew not to tell my mom a word of what we'd just discussed, but it was unnecessary.

"I was just about to show Nova my dress for tonight."

We had a full day of girl talk and primping, and by the time my mother had pinned the last of the tiny white perennials into my hair, I was so nervous I could barely breathe.

I regretted not being able to convince Rose to fully get ready at my house. She was too committed to having a big reveal when she arrived at the ceremony.

From the small glimpse of her dress I got, I understood why. I'd even felt a flare of jealousy when I saw how the bottom of it moved when she swayed in it. I'd been so overwhelmed with the ceremony and getting ready that I'd let Rose walk out of here wearing my ring. I made a mental note to get it back from her before the festivities started. The last thing I needed was for Lan to see someone else wearing the ring he'd just given me.

"It's time to get going." My mother said outside my door.

I appreciated her giving me a moment alone to gather my thoughts.

I looked in the mirror one last time, trying to envision myself in silver. I might've stayed and looked longer if I had known then that the next time I saw myself, I'd be a monster.

CASTOR

I pulled my hood lower as I wandered through The Garden just after sunset. I didn't want to risk being seen, not until I was expected to arrive at the Totem Ceremony with my family. I should have already been at the palace getting ready, but if this was going to be my last time seeing the Totem Ceremony, I wanted to experience every second of it.

The Garden hung beneath the light blue-ish haze of the dying sun, but its beauty only grew with the darkening sky as delicate lanterns filled with flickering light glowed brighter. My mother used to tell me they each held a fairy inside, but now as I looked at them, all I could think about was my banishment and her part in it.

I came up to a row of houses tucked into the trees. Warm laughter and joy spilled out the windows as the tributes prepared for their placement.

I stopped when I spotted Nova seated at a vanity, her mother pinning white flowers into her hair. She was a vision. Undoubtedly charging toward her destiny as a Sylph and as my brother's wife. Sure, some of the tributes wouldn't get into the Totem they wanted, but they'd come to accept it eventually. I followed the glowing lanterns to The Centrum, where hundreds of gardeners were already gathered.

The stadium-esque valley was at the base of the forest. The valley was natural, but the stones had been shaped into stadium seating by several retired Gin hundreds of years ago. I'd hated the Totem ceremony for as long as I could remember. For one, I thought the gardeners should have been allowed to choose their Totems. Second, I despised the formality of the whole thing. The dressing up, the trumpets, the spectacle. The only part I truly enjoyed was the dances.

I couldn't help but notice that it all seemed grander than usual. Had it always been so vibrant, or was I just getting nostalgic? The forest twinkled with the light of the lanterns as if the sun had shattered into tiny pieces and landed like snowflakes scattered across the forest.

I hid among the other gardeners as the tributes arrived one by one, all dressed in white. The air was filled with excitement as the crowd vied to get a peek at the nervous arrivals. I made it my job to know each of the beautiful women of The Garden, but they were hardly recognizable all dolled up for the ceremony. I spotted Rose as she breezed in with a layered dress, followed by some of the male tributes. I liked Rose for her chattiness, though I could only handle her in small doses. She was a stark contrast to the stifled and formal interactions that were forced on us inside the palace. It might have been her nervousness, but Rose's calm demeanor made her appear more womanly and statuesque compared to her usual silly girlishness. She smiled and waved, and I traced her gaze to Nova. Though equally stunning, she looked like she was about to either pass out or throw up, but whatever Rose muttered to her seemed to ease her a bit.

Trumpets blared, indicating the arrival of the royal family. My family. *Shit*. I sprinted around the stadium seating across from the gardeners to where my father, mother, and brother entered. I didn't dare make eye contact with my mother, but Lan's smirk implied I was probably a dead man walking. We sat at our thrones, across from the people and I took in the incredible view of the stage.

There was a girlish giggle among the crowd as Philandro and I took our seats beside our parents. My father rose, silencing the crowd with a single gesture, the entire Centrum granting him their full attention.

"Welcome to this year's placement, a tradition kept in the Garden for more than 10,000 years."

My attention moved to the thirty or so tributes as they lined up next to the stage, and when I saw Nova, I couldn't help but check to see if Lan had spotted her. Sure enough, he was entranced, and I didn't blame him. Even among the angelic tributes, she stood out. I could feel how much was riding on her Totem placement. Loving her was the most rebellious thing Lan had ever done. I hoped for his sake she made Sylph, and that it was enough to win over our parents. Going off his submissive silence at dinner, I wasn't sure Lan had the balls to disobey them.

The King continued. "By Sol, we are all interconnected."

I smiled. I'd heard this speech so many times I could recite it. I was certain the other gardeners could too, but now that this was the last time, I was content to listen.

"The Totems have tasked the people of this Garden to protect the earth below. Today we have thirty-six tributes before us that will become guardians before our eyes."

I felt like some of the youngest gardeners, who

were seeing the ceremony for the first time: full of wonder and excitement.

"The guardians before you are all dressed in white, but will perform a dance to reveal their true souls to the Totems. The Totems will then shroud them in the colors of their true placement. Green represents the Zoi: guardians of earth's life, plants, and animals. Blue is the Atmos: guardians of earth's oceans, lakes, and rivers."

The tributes began to shift nervously. You could almost pick out which placement they were after solely based on their movements when my father called out the name of each totem.

Father's voice filled every inch of The Garden. "Brown, which represents the Gin: guardians of earth's mountains, deserts, and valleys. And finally, silver which represents the Sylphs: guardians of the wind, sky, and stars."

And let's not forget to add in the hellhole they're shipping me off to.

The King stroked his white beard. "Remember that we are here not for the spectacle of this ceremony but for a greater cause. The protection of this world lies in the hands of the guardians. Our ten-year service is a minor price to pay for the continued prosperity of this world."

I burned with envy. What was a mere ten-year service when I was banished for eternity? My royal blood, my immortality, had amounted to nothing but a prison sentence, and now I was left to clasp to the last moments I had. Did my parents hate me that much? Was there no one who loved me even a little?

I'd drowned out the rest of my father's speech, only snapping back to the moment when the first tribute took his position. I didn't know him. He was tall, lanky, and inconsequential for my purposes. He was the kind of person I'd previously overlooked, but in that moment, I envied him. A rush of energy pushed through The Centrum, and we could feel the Totems among us. I held my breath in anticipation, waiting for the music to start and for the first tribute's destiny to be sealed.

NOVA

I forced myself not to make eye contact with Philandro, but I felt his gaze burning my warm cheeks. His presence unnerved me and I couldn't bear the thought of him watching me fail. I leaned forward to get a glimpse of Rose but her gaze was locked on the king, but thankfully, I'd gotten my ring back from her before the ceremony officially started. She didn't seem as nervous as I felt. Hadn't it been Rose who went on for months about how she'd die if she wasn't placed in the Atmos totem? Where was that girl? Why wasn't anyone else freaking out?

I felt sweat begin to slip down the back of my neck. When did I get so sticky? Could everyone tell I was sweating? I fiddled with my ring, wondering if Lan could see it from his place on the stage. The centrum started spinning around me and I willed myself to hold it together just in time for Rory, a tall boy from the east side to step onto the stage. Thank Sol I didn't have to go first, or else the totems would have to place me based on my mad puking skills.

I held my breath as Rory stepped forward; a dull glow radiated off his white suit. It could have been the glow of the lanterns but it looked as if his clothes were dipped in starlight. The music began, and Rory's movements started with several strong kicks. His arms were angular and precise. He squatted down, lifted a single leg in a thrusting kick. His feet were flexed and rigid. He punched his fists forward as if attacking. The music swelled from the forest matching his warrior-like cadence. The drums pounded away rhythmically. Rory was a slender boy, lanky and quiet, but you couldn't tell by watching him dance. In that moment, he was an immovable force. A gasping noise wisped past me prompting me to tear my gaze from Rory. I spotted Leon, one of Rory's closest friends, leaning forward to get a good view. Leon gaped at Rory, as if surprised by the skillful display. I'd be willing to bet based on that reaction that Rory was more in the zone than talented.

The stadium erupted with whispers, snapping my attention back to Rory. It was unmistakable. The bottom of his pantsuit and his sleeves by his wrists had darkened. The color spread like vines in a thickly wooded forest, up to his knee, then over his thigh. It wasn't until it reached his elbows that I could tell it was the deep, rich, brown of the Gin. Rory's dance came to a strong pose and the music ended, just as the last of his white suit, the part by the top of his bowtie, turned brown. The crowd stared, stunned for a moment, silently observing his transformed suit. Aside from its color, it had altered shape as well to appear more angular and structured, with geometric points jutting from the shoulders and the elbows.

The king rose. "The Totems have spoken! Guardian Rory, will now and forever be Gin!"

The crowd burst into cheers, partially for Rory's placement, but mostly for the spectacle of the whole event. It was clear from Rory's bright smile and Leon's nearly hysteric applause, that this outcome was desired. I smiled as I watched him celebrate. I hoped that all the Guardians would be placed where they wanted--but that wasn't the case. In fact, twelve guardian dances later, it was Leon's turn.

Leon's music and dance style was similar to Rory's. He was a much shorter boy than Rory but more solid and muscular. He squatted down and thrust his kicks upward, the same way Rory did but it seemed unnatural. I could see Leon's mother in the crowd, her hands covering her face, but I could tell she was watching through her fingers. Suddenly Leon spun. It was different from Rory's strong pivots. It was angelic and beautiful and unlike any of the other movements he'd done before. There was an audible sigh when he spun a second time. Each spin was lovelier than the last. His suit began to change, but unlike the others it didn't get darker, but brighter.

My stomach sank. It was unmistakable. *Silver,* I mouthed. The crowd gasped as the shiny metallic color spread across Leon's suit. Sylphs were rarely chosen, it had been many ceremonies since anyone had seen one dance. At the end of the dance, Leon stood breathlessly in Silver. Small stars hovered over the suit as if they were orbiting it. The garden shook with applause, many of the onlookers patted his mother on the shoulder in congratulations. I stared at Leon's mother whose hands had lowered to cover only her mouth and chin, but she wasn't joyful. I traced her gaze to Leon.

I swallowed a lump in my throat. Leon stared down at his shiny suit with a look of absolute panic then at Rory who looked equally shocked and somber.

Before the king could even announce Leon's placement I had gone through a myriad of emotions—the major ones being shock, then envy, then rage.

The king hushed the crowd with a wave of his enormous hand. "Citizens of the garden. We have the special privilege to witness the Totem's selection of a Sylph today. Congratulations, Leon."

Leon nodded, biting down on his bottom lip to stop himself from crying. Then he took his place among the others already selected. I tried to cheer for him, but instead my tongue stuck to the back of my throat, and no matter how hard I tried, my body felt too heavy to smile. For the first time, I felt something dark quivering inside me, something that had never been present before. I tried to suppress it, but even as Rose took the attention of the Centrum, glittering in her white gown, I couldn't wipe the scowl from my face or the bitter taste from my mouth.

Rose moved with the grace of a ballerina. Studied and accurate, fluid and graceful. If I was in a normal state I would have had a new view of Rose moving forward. All guardians had to dance for their placement. Many of them practiced for years perfecting their technique, but Rose was a dancer. We were all captivated by the way she could stand on the point of her toes and spin. She lifted one leg into the air, pointing her toe at the sky, her dress fanned from one leg to the other. It splashed back and forth with the rhythm of a wave. As she moved her dress thinned, catching the air more than before. It revealed her slender legs, like two pale blue wings, carrying her across the candlelit stage. The blueness spread, almost white at the bottom of her airy gown to a deep blue at the top of her chest.

Applause filled the air as Rose struck her final pose, on her tiptoes with both arms beautifully curved above her head. Her skirt swirled around her, as if still dancing. I couldn't help but sneak a peek at Philandro. Had he been impressed by Rose's dance? I felt a pang of guilt. Philandro wasn't staring at Rose, he was staring at me. Actually, I noticed, quite a few of the people in the Centrum were. Was it my face? Was I not smiling? My attention snapped back to Rose. This was Rose's moment. Rose had wanted Atmos and there she was standing in blue. But a new wave of anxious energy slammed me. *Why can't I just be happy for her?* All I could think about was Leon—how he'd ungratefully accepted his position as a Sylph--My position. What were the odds that they'd choose two Sylphs in one year? They couldn't be good. Perhaps it wasn't impossible. I was too immersed in thought to notice the king announcing Rose's placement in the Atmos or the thunderous applause that followed. In fact I didn't think of Rose at all until she was standing directly in front of me.

"Huh?" I said suddenly crashing back to reality.

"Why didn't you clap for me?" Rose whispered as

she passed. Before I could answer she sat with the other Atmos.

I was relieved. I had no answer. Was that why people were staring? They'd looked at Rose's closest friend for a reaction and I hadn't reacted? Was that what Lan was thinking too? But there was no time to figure it out, no time to apologize. It was my turn to dance.

PHILANDRO

As Nova took her first position, I contemplated whether I should watch or not. The pressure must've been immense, but there was nothing I could do to help her now. Her hands crossed at the wrists above her head and I turned to Castor, but his gaze was fixed on Nova, his dark eyes glaring down at her. He nodded slowly, knowingly and I could feel how badly he wanted her to succeed. Despite our differences, he always managed to be a great brother. Nova's gaze rose to meet Castor's and the back of my neck burned hot. A small smile played at her lips and I could have sworn that something secret had transpired between them. *Was it in my head?* Nova tore her gaze away just as the music began soft and smooth.She brought her arms down and spun. She tossed her arms outward and lunged slowly to the right; she stepped back. The melody reminded me of one Castor used to play on the flute when we were kids.

Castor's expression revealed very little. He was completely focused on her performance. Nova's movements deepened as she lunged down, letting her arms fall back behind her. She lifted her body to the sky chest first, weaving her arms through the air. As the music took her, she began to look sultry. She spun, her white glittering gown swirling around her, swishing against her legs just as the edges of her dress started to change. Her dress glowed yellow-ish in the candlelight and it swayed, it looked like it was on fire where it met the ground. The orange glow travelled up her skirt in an uneven ring, almost too slowly to notice. It rose, leaving behind a very distinct color. I shifted in my throne as the crowd began to whisper above the music.

"Is it Gin?" I whispered to Castor, but despite it's dark color vaguely resembling the brown that marked the Gin Totem, it was notably different.

Castor confirmed my fears when he shook his head and whispered. "It's black."

The charcoal color spread like leftover coals once the ring of fire passed. It burned past her waist, and over her chest, leaving a lacy black top. It dipped to a deep v shape almost to her bellybutton, revealing much of her chest, but the fiery glow didn't stop there. It latched onto her sunshine blonde hair turning it to a deep blood red. Just as Nova finished her last move and the music came to an end, fire stained her lips a deep crimson red. Castor stood, but I was frozen. The audience watched, their whispers now a roar of concern, waiting to hear the King's announcement.

Still out of breath from her dance, Nova's chest rose and fell. Her gaze fixed to Castor. I turned to him and his expression said it all, with widened eyes—his mouth agape. Nova's gaze dropped to her dress as someone in the crowd shrieked with fear.

"B-Black?" Nova mouthed. She turned to the crowd as their panic began to sink into her and into me at the same time. I needed to act, to find out what was happening, but I was paralyzed—struck motionless by the sight of this new person standing before me. She looked so different without her golden hair. Those red lips were not the soft pink ones I'd kissed.

In all the ceremonies since the beginning of the garden there had never been a Guardian who finished their dance wearing black. What did it mean?

Nova stood in the middle of the Centrum as the entire garden judged her, myself included. The moment dragged until finally my father rose. Before he even got the words out, Nova's first tears started to fall.

The king didn't need to hush the crowd, he already had their full attention.

"Ladies and Gentlemen of the Garden, don't be alarmed. I urge you to open your minds as I explain to you what we've all just witnessed. We should not fear the unknown, but rather seek it. It alone holds the trials necessary for personal growth, like a wave smoothing stones with it's pressure and greatness." He scanned the crowd.

"I have begun training my eldest son Price Philandro to take my place as king. This process has caused me to reflect on my time as ruler of the garden and protector of the world below. I've noticed a realm that I've previously ignored. I'd always assumed it to be barren and without life, but I was quite wrong. This land has become unruly and in dire need of guidance. I have bestowed a king-hood to my youngest song Prince Castor, to oversee this unknown land henceforth. The garden, sensing this new realm under our dominion, has selected it's first guardian to protect it. And so it gives me great pleasure to announce that Nova has been selected to become the first ever Nymph of the Underworld."

A nymph totem? That's impossible. There was no applause. Instead, the Centrum filled with a weighted silence. The candle lit faces of the other gardeners stared at Nova. I turned to Castor who fell back into his throne, the look of defeat confirming what my father had said to be true. Why hadn't he told me? He was leaving the garden forever? No wonder he'd been acting so strange. How did I not see this coming?

"Father, you have to do something," I said, but he only looked down on Nova with pity. "You can't send Castor away like this," I said.

I felt for Nova, but I was having a hard time reconciling the girl dressed in black and the girl I'd known like the back of my hand. The garden didn't make mistakes. A placement revealed the true nature of a person. Even in my astonishment I knew that it must have been I who had been mistaken about Nova. My little brother on the other hand was another story. He was assigned a life in the Underworld. He'd been cursed with this decision and hadn't even come to me. I reached for him, grabbing his forearm. "Castor."

He pulled his arm away.

"Castor! Wha—"

His cold glare silenced me, before it returned to the Centrum where I caught one last glance at Nova before she bounded from the stadium into the woods. Bound by duty, I had no choice but to stay put, and for the rest of the ceremony, but all I could think about

BRITTNI CHENELLE

was Nova leaping from the edge of the garden with no intention of calling her dragon to catch her.

When I turned back to Castor I could see the same fear in his intense gaze, but unlike me, my brother was less concerned with obligation, and for once, I was glad for it. "Go," I muttered under my breath. His eyes lit and without needing more, he did what I couldn't. He sprang from his throne and chased her into the darkness.

NOVA

The branches of the forest lashed at me as I raced through it, my body craving more speed as if I could outrun the ceremony, my placement, and my entire damnation to hell. It has to be a mistake. But the thought was too blasphemous to reach my lips. The Garden suddenly felt too small, the air too thin. My finger stung with pain from where Lan's ring had burned off my finger into ash. My foot caught on a root and I stumbled, glancing back to see where I misstepped, only to lose balance completely. I slammed down to the mud that squished beneath me, my sudden stop spilling crimson locks into my face, like blood poured over my head. I braced myself for the tears, but I felt numb—completely detached from my body.

A low voice hummed in the darkness. "I'm sorry this happened to you."

I lept to my feet, my eyes scanning the shadows until I saw Castor standing a few feet away. His face was turned away from me, his dark hair covering his eyes as he waited for me to address him.

My heart raced as the words shot out. "It's a mistake. It must be."

He chuckled softly, "Denouncing the Totems are we? Who will you pray to now, Satan? Not a bad idea considering."

"Is this funny to you?" I snapped. "I suppose you're fine with going to the Underworld then?"

Castor's gaze met mine. "You can at least take comfort in knowing that the Totems are never wrong."

"Does that mean you believe the king is wrong about you?"

"Not anymore," he said, his gaze loaded with whisperings as it fixed on me.

Tears of frustration slipped from my eyes and I swiped at them. Here I was trying to cope with the loss of everything I've ever wanted and Castor was gloating about not being damned alone. "I am not going to the Underworld to keep you company—in fact, I'm not going at all."

He stepped closer. "You misunderstand me. It's not your companionship that puts me at ease but rather the surprising nature of your placement."

"Then you agree I don't belong there."

He tilted his head, the moonlight peeking through the trees and finding his eyes. "I think that perhaps our job in the Underworld could also prove to be unexpected."

I exhaled my frustration. He wasn't going to convince me to be happy about this. I had to find a way to change my placement. "Where's Lan?"

Castor nodded, as if he'd been expecting the question, his gaze moving back to ground. "He had to stay for the end of the ceremony."

"And you didn't?"

He shrugged, "I'm already damned."

I shook my head. "He should be here. I need to talk to him."

"Look Nova, it's a lot to take in. Give him some time."

Dread pooled at the bottom of my stomach, "Did he say something to you?"

He shook his head. "No. But he's a very traditional person. All of this is new territory."

I stared as Castor kicked at a rock. I'd lost Lan. A wave of sadness threatened to spill from my eyes, the humiliation unbearable.

"I-I need to go home," I said, finally.

"I'll walk you," Castor said matter of factly. I

didn't have the will to refuse, so I dusted myself off and started the slow trudge toward my house, hoping Castor would let me suffer in silence.

Castor cleared his throat. "I'm not good at handling situations like this. I don't really know what to say."

I cringed, but the trees had done well to block out most of the moonlight, hiding my face enough to avoid insulting the prince. My thoughts moved back to my placement. Castor must've known about the Underworld before the ceremony. Come to think of it, he was kind of sulking the last time I'd seen him. At the time, I'd assumed he was just like that. Everyone knew he was broody and mysterious—exactly the type I would expect as the lord of the Underworld—but me? By the Sol, how did the totem get this so wrong? I was no more suited to be there than Philandro himself.

Realizing Castor was waiting for a response, I asked, "Have you been there—to the Underworld, I mean?"

He pressed his lips together. "No. I was uh, going to check it out the other day when you attacked me."

I smiled with the corner of my mouth. "Rescued."

"Ah, that's right. Rescued."

I felt a touch of comfort as my house came into view at the edge of the forest. Light poured from the windows and I could hear a soft bustle of movement inside. The ceremony must've ended. I turned to Castor, "Thanks for walking me."

He nodded, his eye-contact lingering as if he'd wanted to say something else but thought better of it. He turned back to the forest. "Castor!" I called.

He stopped but didn't turn back.

"And thanks for coming to check on me."

I turned back to my home, gripping the handle as I pictured the warmth of my mother's embrace. But as I turned the knob, it didn't move--the door was locked. Bewildered, I raised my fist and knocked instead. The bustle inside went quiet. I knocked again, knowing I'd be heard this time. "Mom!" I called, knocking louder, a touch of desperation slipping into my voice. "Mom! It's me." The door cracked open and I pushed, but it didn't budge.

I noticed a wisp of my mom's hair through the crack, as she leaned against the door and whispered, "Do you know what they're saying? They're calling you a demon."

"Let me in mom."

"I'm sorry," she whispered, the door closing between us.

I stumbled back. "Mom," I gasped, "it's me."

The door remained closed in front of me as a

strange sensation built inside of me, threatening to erupt. I could feel it all—everything I'd lost in a matter of minutes: my dream, my home, my mom, Lan, my appearance, even Rose. It rose up my throat, unstoppable like a team of horses, galloping toward the light.

My shoulders shook and my head rocked back as a fit of laughter tore through me. Once I started I couldn't stop. I clutched my stomach, my body surging with glee as my life burned down around me. Tears of catharsis ran down my face. It wasn't funny, but it felt so good to surrender to the errant emotion.

A branch snapped and I turned to see Castor, staring wide eyed at me. The look on his face only made me laugh harder. I doubled over.

"Well," he chuckled, " at least it can't get any worse."

Tears dribbled off my chin, my stomach aching until I could finally take a breath. "And why did my hair color change?" I asked, prompting another bout of laughter.

"I like it," Castor said through bursts. "You probably don't know this, but your lips are red too."

I snorted. "You're kidding."

He grinned. I took several slow breaths, the jovial feeling leaving me only with grief. "I'm a monster," I said.

Castor exhaled through his nose. "Alright, monster. Let's go."

"Where?"

"You can crash at my place," he said, waving me over.

"The Palace?" I asked.

Castor shrugged and headed into the moonlit forest. The Palace? It was too strange a concept to fully comprehend. Was he even permitted to invite me to the palace? Would I see Philandro there? I followed Castor back into the woods, trying not to resent his obvious pity—or perhaps, knowing that he wouldn't be alone in the Underworld brought him more comfort than he cared to admit, because if I was honest, it did the same for me.

PHILANDRO

My thoughts raced like a sky dragon slipping through bouts of wind like silk. Why hadn't Castor told me about the Underworld? I paced around my room, the fireplace a metronome of time—tormenting me with each pop and crackle of its embers.

My thoughts filled with flashes of red hair and lips, the black lacy gown that had pulled Nova so suddenly out of my reach. Whoever that girl was, it wasn't Nova. Not the girl whose hair was sunshine and bright eyes were always cast to the sky. I knew better than to doubt the Totems, but something wasn't adding up. Either Nova had fooled me for a lifetime, or I'd missed something. The ceremony replayed in my head, different details springing to the forefront each time. Then I saw Nova's eyes, as they focused on Castor, the seductive swing of Nova's hips as her dance began.

"Brother," Castor said, startling me from my thoughts. I turned to see him closing the door behind him. He sighed, observing me like he could see the seeds of doubt that sprouted to entangle my chest with carnivorous plants. He took a seat beside the fire. Rubbing his hands and holding them out to the light.

"Did you find her?" I asked, my impatience growing.

He nodded, not bothering to turn his face to me. "She's staying in one of the guest rooms."

"In the palace? You can't be serious."

"Her mother didn't let her in. All of the gardeners think she's some kind of monster."

"Can't you understand why?"

He chuckled, the reaction irking me as I took a seat across from him. "I'm afraid I can't," he said finally.

I breathed into my hands. "That red hair, the black dress—"

"So this is about appearance then? It's not like she asked for this."

"Of course not. She'd look beautiful no matter what. It's what this all represents. Those dances reveal our true inner nature. What do you think it means that she's going to be sent there? It's about everything. Did you see the way she danced? The way her eyes filled with lust. The Totems saw what I couldn't—something dark in her, something evil. To be the first one ever to be selected for such a placement... I don't know who that person is."

Castor's lack of response drew my attention to him, but he only stared blankly at the fire. I straightened. "Cas, I'm sorry. I didn't mean—"

"It's too late for that. I don't know Nova well enough to speak for her, but I wouldn't describe myself in those exact terms."

"I didn't mean you," I said, quickly.

He stood slowly, stretching his arms over his head. "The funny thing is, I was starting to come to terms with father's decision. I thought perhaps, there was more to the Underworld than what meets the eye and that I might enjoy being the first to uncover it." His cold gaze landed on me like a steel ax. "But if my brother, the noble and just Philandro, sees no merit in the fifth Totem, or anyone sent there, I've stumbled into a cruel fate indeed."

He headed for the door.

"You can't possibly want to go. Tell me the truth."

He stopped with his hand on the doorknob, before he said, "If you plan to use all of your influence to rescue someone from the Underworld, perhaps it should be the woman you confessed your feelings to not ten hours ago."

"Cas," I called, but he'd already disappeared into the hallway, leaving me with the wounds he'd inflicted so politely.

I balled my fist in frustration, the Underworld conjuring images of death, demons, evil in my head. All manor of lore had agreed it was a place to be despised and avoided. I didn't believe for a second that Castor wanted to rule there. He was most likely putting on a brave face, as usual, and I'd just spit in it. *What's wrong with me?*

Even his point about Nova rang true. What kind of man could turn his back on the woman he loved, especially when she needed me the most? In all this I hadn't even considered what she must be going through.

I pondered those questions until the fireplace had gone cold and quiet, but instead of finding answers, they only held me from drifting off to sleep like an anchor.

I had to see Nova.

I pulled myself from my bed, slipping a shirt on before I moved silently into the hallway. Making my way to the guest rooms, I felt a war range inside me. A war of what was proper and appropriate, versus what my body felt compelled to do.

My pulse intensified as I approached the next

hallway as sinister shadows shrouded the doors in blackness. I planned to knock on each door until I found Nova's room. Once inside, I'd listen to her side of things before making a decision. But as I approached the first door, I heard a sniffle on the other side. I froze, my head fogging as I listened for another. She sniffed again, the soft sound sending every beautiful memory I had of her slinging back. Before I could think better of it—before I could consider my position, propriety, or what her Totem meant for us—I opened the door and slipped inside, my eyes locking on the moonlit figure as her tearful eyes met mine. Then, as if I knew every sinful act that would follow, I locked the door behind me.

NOVA

I hesitated before entering the palace for the first time, reluctant to give up the wonders I'd conjured about it as a child for mere reality, but the palace didn't disappoint. The natural materials were smoothed to a shine, the beads of my gown making a pleasing sprinkling sound as they ran along the marble floors. The candlelight from the chandeliers caught flecks of gold that rimmed the carved archways. Castor looked back at me over his shoulder more than once, as if he feared I'd run, but I had nowhere to go—nowhere to hide on the island which now felt like it shrank with every unsteady breath I took.

"Wait here," Castor said, dipping behind a pair of double doors. I exhaled, trying to find a distraction to my discomfort. I drank in the intricacies of the murals as they sung stories across every surface. Beautiful winged people reaching toward the sun's light. My gaze traveled down, to lush forests with doe-eyed animals that seemed to be moving along the forest floor. Finally I crouched, leaning closer as my gaze moved toward the floor. There I saw a single man depicted, his face turned up to the sky, his mouth twisted in agony as demon-like creatures consumed him into a swarm of taloned claws and bloodthirsty teeth. I swallowed a mouthful of fear, as I traced my hand over his face, my hand shaking as I stared into my future.

"Nova."

My breath skipped as Castor reached a hand to me. I took it and he pulled me upright, before nodding for me to follow him. I tried to keep my focus on him, but the murals—teeth and claws followed us, snarling at me from the shadowed corners of the hall. Castor stopped outside a door.

"A selection of clothes will be brought in the morning. There's a nightgown ready in the closet."

"Thank you," I murmured. I reached for the door, but Castor's hand stopped me.

He sighed. "I know things seem bad, but I'm sure they'll look better in the morning." He shrugged. "They're just murals."

I nodded my thanks and disappeared into the room, desperate to hide myself away before the tears started. I headed straight for the closet, when I caught a glimpse of myself in the vanity mirror across the room. I ran to it, tears spilling from my cheeks as terror consumed me. Had the Totem just torn out my heart, and used it to dye my hair and lips? I looked fierce—demonic—my dress the color of burned sulfur. I strained to pull it off, desperate to peel the cursed garment away. I tossed it on the floor, stomping on it for good measure as I pulled helplessly at my hair. The transformation was severe. It was no wonder my mother didn't welcome me back, it was no wonder the entire garden thought I was a monster. I undeniably looked the part. I opened the closet where the night-gown Castor had promised hung. It was white, the color that held so many promises. I slipped it on, then climbed into bed, the softness of it startling me as I sank into it. It felt good to cry, to mourn the loss of my dream.

The door swung open and Lan stepped inside. I froze as the lock clicked behind him.

Moonlight poured into the room through four arched windows, sending Lan through ribbons of light and darkness as he crossed the room to me.

"Lan," I breathed. "I'm so sorry." My voice hitched as he took a seat beside me on the bed, heat flooding my body as he stared down at a strand of crimson hair between his fingers. A wave of shame assaulted me.

"How did this happen?" he said, shattering my heart into keen shards.

"I... I don't know. I'm afraid Lan."

His honey-colored gaze moved to meet mine, but he quickly turned away. "That dance," he whispered.

"I don't know what to say. I practiced, I put my whole heart into it, even Castor helped me improve—"

"What did you say?"

His harsh tone sent a prickling sensation over my skin. "I practiced."

"Castor helped you with your dance?"

I swallowed my words.

His eyes lit. "That's it. By helping he altered your placement. I knew you didn't belong in the Nymph Totem." He stood. "I can fix this."

He charged toward the door, closing it behind him and leaving me alone with my jumbled thoughts. I didn't intend on throwing Castor to the wolves, after all he was the one who'd come to my rescue, but for the first time since my placement I felt the flutterings of hope. Maybe Lan was right, maybe it was a mistake. If Castor hadn't helped me I would be in Sylph.

The door swung open and Lan rushed back in, pulling a shirtless Castor along with him. I turned my gaze to the window trying to look anywhere but at Castor's bare chest, his rippled abs distractingly ringing in my ears like the morning bells. My cheeks burned as the pair of princes crossed the room.

"Sorry, I don't do threesomes with my brother in them," Castor said.

I stole a quick eyeful. That's a damn shame. I appreciated the mood-breaker, but Lan didn't pause to acknowledge Castor's joke. "Tell me exactly what happened."

"What's all this about?" Castor asked.

I allowed my gaze to move to him again. "Well, I saw someone jump from the cliff and I ran to help, but it was only Castor. We got tangled up and landed on Earth. Then Castor asked me to show him my routine and he gave me some tips."

My heartbeat seemed almost audible as Castor's eyes narrowed. "What are you talking about?"

"The other day," I said, confusion starting to settle in.

Castor's brow furrowed. "The first time I ever saw you dance was at the ceremony."

I was struck silent by the blatant lie, but he didn't stop there.

"Oh I see, you're trying to get out of your placement by using me as an excuse."

"N-no. That's—Why are you lying?"

Lan stood, his gaze moving between us.

"You have to believe me. Please, Lan." I shuddered at the slow rise and fall of Lan's chest as he considered whether or not I'd made the whole thing up. "Please," I begged.

Lan placed a hand on Castor's shoulder then turned away. He headed for the door, leaving me to sink into a inferno of anger and disbelief. The door closed behind him, my attention turning to Castor whose mischievous grin made my blood boil. A dark shadow cast over my eyes as my instincts took over and I lunged at him.

CASTOR

A mess of fiery hair and limbs collided with me. Nova pulled me down to the bed, and I bit back a smile as I tried to wrestle her back into submission. Her punches were weak and growing weaker as she tired herself out, but her anger was understandable. Both Lan and Nova were looking for an excuse to doubt the Totems, and I was their scapegoat. The gardeners always helped each other with their dances, and it had never affected the Totems before. Lan was blinded by his love for her. That was all. The last thing I needed was for him to get lost in an obsessive and fruitless quest to 'rescue' Nova from her rightful placement.

Nova grunted an indistinguishable sound of frustration as she slapped uselessly at my back, her silk-thin sleep dress doing little to conceal her body as she thrashed against me. I shivered, my body responding in all the wrong ways to what I was sure she meant as a punishment. Her gaze met mine, and in them, I saw something new. Something formidable yet familiar. It was a look I'd never seen from her before. Hot and reckless. Something that felt connected to her Totem. Finally, she sighed, letting herself go limp. I stood and backed away as a rush of guilt slammed into me. I didn't know why I found myself so suddenly attracted to her after her placement. She'd always seemed plain to me before, and now I couldn't take my eyes off her. I shook the thought from my head. She was Philandro's girl, and that was a line I knew I'd never cross. *By the Sol, please don't say I let that factor into my decision to lie.*

Tears slipped from her eyes. "Why did you lie?"

"Your placement was not a mistake, Nova. You need to come to grips with it. I can't have you bringing my brother down fighting the actual Totems because you don't like your placement."

"I hate you."

Her words were like steel, striking me harder than any of the physical blows she'd taken, though I wasn't sure exactly why.

"I can live with that," I said, heading for the door.

"Get out!" she shouted, but I had already reached the far side of the room.

"With pleasure," I called back before slamming the door behind me.

I stewed all the way back to my room. She hated *me*? No. I hated her. She walked around this place like she was the only one dissatisfied with their placement. I'd wager half of the gardeners were. She wasn't special. She wasn't even the only one being sent to the Underworld. I'd done nothing but support her, and of course, I was the bad guy for telling one little lie to protect them both. She was nothing but a brat. I hated everything, from the way she fawned over Lan to her sexy red lips. Those lips kept me up half the night. The other half was lost to the feel of her curves against my body with nothing but that thin little nightgown between us.

I sat at the breakfast table, running my finger around the rim of my glass as I tried in vain to block the whole night from my thoughts.

Lan startled me from my efforts when he took a seat beside me. A server placed his breakfast in front of him.

He eyed me. "You look unwell," he said as he began to eat. "Something on your mind?"

As a matter of fact. Yes. Guilt, mostly. For lying and for being attracted to your girlfriend.

"No."

A whisper in the hallway drew both of our attention. A moment later, a server guided Nova to a seat across from us. Her hair was pinned up off her shoulders, her dress structured and form-fitting and the purple color only made her hair color look more ridiculous. I stared down at my plate.

An insufferable silence dragged as a plate was placed in front of Nova until Philandro broke it. "You look nice today, Nova," he said.

I choked on my water. *Now, who's the liar?* I waved their attention away.

Lan leaned forward. "I've given it some thought, and I understand you must've been under a lot of stress yesterday. I forgive you for lying."

"Thank you, your highness," she said softly.

"I was surprised not to see you at the cliffs this morning," he added.

She stared down at her plate. "I wasn't feeling up to it."

Lan reached out and held her hands at the center of the table. My stomach turned.

"Listen, Nova. We can get through this. I still want to be with—"

A servant cleared their throat at the door before announcing the King and Queen. I'd never in my life been so glad for my parents' arrival. After the King and Queen sat down, everyone settled into polite conversation. Nova played the role of demure victim as she wilted before us, and Lan ate it up. He finally had a damsel to rescue, and even with my lie, I was sure by the end of the meal that he had already thought up a plan to get Nova's placement reversed.

Time was on my side, though. In just three days, the placements would begin. I'd take my place in the Underworld alongside Nova, and all I had to do to make it happen was fan the flames and wait for the real Nova to reveal herself.

NOVA

I could do nothing except go through the motions and say the right things. I spent my time trying to prove to Philandro that I was the same girl he'd loved not a full day ago. But something inside of me had changed. The part of me that had loved Lan's sense of justice. The part of him who believed he'd stand by me—and if I was honest, my entire routine seemed to fit me as well as my life in the palace. I was walking on eggshells in constant terror that everything could be torn away in an instant. I was angry. Angry at the Totems for my placement, angry at my mother, at Rose, at the garden, and above all, I detested Castor, who'd lied so that he wouldn't have to endure banishment alone. Of everyone's part in my misfortunes, his was the only bit of it that was intentionally cruel, and I couldn't even look him in the eye without my skin burning hot. I stood on the edge of the cliffs, my hair whipping in the wind as I searched for the certainty to thrust myself off the edge, but the routine that had once felt so natural now felt like it belonged to someone else.

Dejected, I turned away from the cliff with every intention of putting my tail between my legs and retreating back to the safety of my palace bedroom. I strode into the forest, feeling like the corseted dress the servants had picked out for me was some kind of cruel joke. My thoughts bucked like wild stallions, distracting me just enough to disorient my sense of direction. I scanned the lush forest, cursing myself for not paying better attention. At this rate, it would take me all afternoon to make it back to the palace, and the last thing I wanted was to run into one of the gardeners and be forced to endure my entire ordeal again from their perspective.

I was saved by the babbling of the waterfall in the distance. It was a great deal out of my way, an hour or so off the trail to the palace, but it was a reliable land-mark. I knew once I found it, I could easily find my way back to the palace. I pushed the brush to the side to get a look at the falls.

My mouth dropped open when I saw Lan at the base of the falls, his head back and his eyes closed as the waterfall poured over his body. I felt the stirrings of something fierce at the pit of my stomach, something that refused to let me look away.

Before I could think better of it, I pushed through the greenery, stepping across the smooth stones at the edge of the clear water where I saw Philandro's clothes laid out. I eyed them: shirt, pants, and undergarments. I turned my attention back to the water where he washed in the nude, my heart racing as if it could outrun what I knew had to come next. Lan could save me. All he needed was to believe in me enough. Castor's lie had put doubt in his mind, but now I had him alone. I had a chance to make an undeniable connection with him that no lie could unravel.

I reached behind me, fumbling for the strings of my dress. I pulled and felt something come loose, then, with effort, I shimmied it down to my ankles and stepped out of it. I considered slipping off my under-wear, but I couldn't muster the courage. Instead, I stepped into the water, the cold shock climbing up my legs.

A hot hand pressed over my lips from behind as someone dragged me back out of the water. I thrashed, my body burning with fear, as my muffled screams were swallowed by the waterfall. "Lan," I screamed, "turn around!"

But my words were lost. Lan held his hands out to the water, oblivious to my cries for help.

Branches clawed at me as I was pulled out of Philandro's field of vision.

"Are you insane?" Castor whispered, still holding my mouth.

I slapped his hands away. "Me? Why the hell did you do that? How did you know I was here?"

He shook his head, "Look. I really believe you belong in the Underworld. I was waiting for proof. Some traits to be amplified, some choices you might not have made before your placement."

My mind sorted through the bullshit. "You followed me... What is wrong with you?"

"It's a good thing I did. Not only did you prove my point with the stunt you were about to pull, but you would have wrecked things with Lan too."

Anger scorched me. "Oh, thank Sol I have you here to protect my virginity."

Castor's cheeks bloomed, and it felt like the word virginity was stuck in the air between us.

I tried to cover it by talking. "You don't understand. Things have been different today. We've connected again."

"You don't see it. Do you? The change has already happened to you. You were about to throw your—"

his gaze trailed down my body, then rose back to my face, "—mostly naked body at Lan. Mr. Propriety himself. Best case scenario he screws you and helps you out of guilt. Worst case, he's horrified by such a brazen move."

I swallowed hard, his words ringing true.

"What he's connecting with is this innocent act you've had on all day."

"It's not an—"

"—Then why are we having this discussion?"

I ran my hands over my face.

"I'm not judging you," Castor said. "Personally, I think it was kind of badass. I would have been into it. But if you want Lan, you have to admit to yourself that yesterday you would have never thought to do something like that, and today you're a bit more...well, like me."

"Fine," I said, my chest heavy with embarrassment.

Castor peeked over the branches. "Shit, he's coming to get his clothes!"

I stood, trying to make a break for it.

"Wait, your dress!"

In a frantic moment, I collided with Castor, and we toppled back through the branches to the edge of the water. Stunned, we froze as a half-dressed Lan stared wide-eyed at us as I peered up at him from under Castor. I reached for my dress, but it was several inches out of my reach.

"Lan, I—"

"Brother," Castor said, standing.

"What is this?" Lan asked, the hurt in his voice wounding me.

Castor helped me to my feet and blocked my body from Lan's view while I tried to think of an explanation. But the truth was just as bad as what he probably thought he'd stumbled upon.

"I came out here to practice my new abilities when I accidentally set Nova's dress on fire. I didn't know she was out here. Luckily she hasn't been hurt."

My gaze moved to my gown, which smoldered with fresh ash. I could see the relief in Philandro's eyes as he handed me his shirt. I slipped quickly into it. How had Castor done that? What abilities did he possess?

Lan wrapped his arm around me. "You really should be more careful, Cas," he said, then turned to address me. "Let's get you back to the palace."

I looked back over my shoulder to see my smoldering dress, laying on the rocks in perfect condition. Was I losing my mind? Hadn't it just been smoking a moment ago? Castor stared after us. He'd lied again, this time to help me. I wondered if guilt had changed his tune, but it didn't matter. I was more certain than ever that he couldn't be trusted. Even so, he had answers. He knew what was happening to me, and if I had any chance of getting Lan back, I had to find out too.

CASTOR

The castle was still and quiet, the moonlight peeking through a gap in the curtains as I lay in my bed. I lifted my hand, staring at it as the flames crawled smoothly over my skin. The sensation was strange, prickly, and unnatural. Without the pain from the heat, it was almost too easy to accidentally set things on fire. If Lan hadn't come to my room last night, I probably would have burned the palace down. The flame snuffed out, and I rolled onto my side. Lan saw the world in black and white, and I couldn't fault him for that. Nova was off-limits, and I had to stop getting myself in dangerous situations with her. I was sure once Lan got over the shock of Nova's placement, he'd come around, maybe even get her placement changed. In the meantime, I just had to keep my distance. It wouldn't be hard. My plate was full.

Philandro had our father to train him, to explain the intricacies of being King of the Garden and the original four totems, but not even Father knew what to expect from the Underworld. I'd read every book I could get my hands on on the subject but most only served to unnerve me, with the exception of one. I eyed the thick tome that sat at a table by the window, deciding instantly that I was too tired to retrieve it when I heard a gentle knock on my door.

I pushed up to my elbows to see Nova peek her head in the room.

"Castor?" she whispered.

"Get out," I said, dropping back into my bed and crossing my arms over my face. *This girl's going to be the death of me.* I squeezed my eyes shut, hoping that would be the end of it, but a moment later, I felt the bed move. I groaned. "What are you doing here?"

Nova sat at the edge of the bed, her hair pulled into one braid that ran down one shoulder like molten lava. "I'm sorry to bother you, but I have some questions."

"Ask me in the morning."

"I can't sleep. Not with all of this uncertainty swirling around my head. Besides, do you really think Lan is going to let me out of his sight after our little incident this afternoon?"

"And how do you think he's going to feel about

you climbing into bed with me in the middle of the night?"

Her gaze fell, and she stood quickly. "You're right. I'm sorry. I shouldn't have come."

That's right. Get out of here before you drag me into more trouble. But the disappointment in the slouch of her shoulders paired with the very recent memory of her telling me she hated me compelled me to speak. "Wait." I sighed, disappointed with my lack of willpower. "What was your question?"

"Will I get abilities like you?" she asked, this time standing a few feet away from my bed rather than sitting on it.

"Most likely. The other totems have some."

"But you don't know for sure," she said, shifting.

I shook my head.

"What *do* you know?"

I tapped the edge of my bed with my hand, and her eyes narrowed before she once again took a seat.

"Since this is a new totem, there's not a lot of information. We can assume we have some job to complete like the others, but the rest is speculation."

She exhaled slowly. "I was afraid of that. So then it could be all hellfire and death." The sadness on her face made me want to touch her.

"Most of the lore says so."

Her eyebrows raised. "Not all?"

I smirked, nodding over to the window. She spotted the book, immediately jumping off the bed and running to it like a child at Christmas. She held it to her chest as she brought it back, her smile fading as she stood beside the bed.

"Can I?" she asked, gesturing to the space beside me.

I moved over, and she plopped down so close it made me shiver. She opened the book on our laps. The citrusy scent of her hair made my face warm, my thoughts glued to her proximity as I stared emptily at the page.

"Okay, so walk me through it."

"I will," I said, my voice cracking with discomfort. "But keep in mind this is just speculation."

"Anything is better than the constant image of hell-fire in my head. Please, Cas? I need to sleep."

Her use of my nickname sent a flare of heat through me so intense and fast that I thought for a moment I'd set us both on fire. "Okay, so, basically, this talks about the Underworld as something pliable. I flipped through the book, pulling up a picture of a cavern filled with glowing gemstones. It's powered with something the book calls essence, but I don't really know where it comes from."

"It's beautiful," she said, her fingertips sweeping over the image. "Tell me more."

* * *

A knock at my door jerked me awake. The harsh white light of day sliced through the gap in my curtains. I looked down to see a mess of red hair and Nova snoring on the pillow beside me, and the book we'd spent the night reading sliding toward the edge of the bed.

"Castor!" Philandro called. "Wake up."

Nova sat up, her eyes going wide as she scrambled to cover herself. "By the Sol, I fell asleep!"

I bit back a laugh watching her scramble for cover despite being fully clothed. The book slammed to the floor, causing Nova to jump and Philandro to knock again.

"What do I do?" Nova whispered. "Why are you laughing? He's going to think something happened."

"But nothing did," I said, standing and striding toward the door.

"Where are you going?" she whisper-yelled.

I looked back over my shoulder. "To get the door, obviously."

I took my time, trying not to laugh as she flailed on

the floor, pulling herself under my bed. I opened the door.

"Brother," I said.

Lan brightened. "There you are. I thought we could go down to the mainland today and stir up a bit of trouble before you have to go. A sort of last hurrah."

"I'm sorry, but I am just about at my limit for trouble these days. Has breakfast been served?"

"Yes, about ten minutes ago." He followed me out into the hallway. "I'll join you, but I still think you should consider my offer. By the way, have you seen Nova this morning?"

"She's under my bed," I said, matter of factly.

NOVA

My stomach dropped when I heard footsteps fast approaching the bed. I squeezed my eyes shut, nearly jumping from my skin as Lan snatched the bedskirt up. I scrambled out from under the bed, my knees scraping against the carpet as Lan backed away, running his hands through his hair and breathing deeply like he was going to drop right where he stood.

"Lan, I can expla—"

"Don't. Please, don't."

I looked up at Castor, who leaned casually against the wall with a smirk that said he didn't care which way this turned out as long as he could watch the fireworks. "Tell him, Castor."

Castor sighed, reluctant to join the fray that he'd so obviously orchestrated. "Brother—"

Lan silenced him with a raise of his hand. I froze as

Lan's honey-colored gaze fell to me, the intensity of his eyes threatening to make me cry right in front of him. My pulse quickened as I braced myself to witness the darkness in him for the first time, my curiosity as hungry for answers as my fear.

I heard Castor say, "Wait, brother, don't—" just as Lan reached for me.

Lan's warm lips found mine, the shock of it knocking me off balance, but it didn't matter. His arms wrapped tightly around me with an intensity I was too stunned to match.

"Shit," Castor said, in a commotion on the other side of the room.

Lan released me, turning back to see Castor trying to stomp some embers out of the curtains.

Lan smiled. "You really should get that under control."

"Sorry," Castor said, giving his smoldering curtain one final stomp. "Didn't mean to wreck your moment or whatever. Think I'll go grab breakfast."

Lan waited for Castor to leave before he turned his attention back to me.

"What was that about?" I asked, still replaying the kiss in my head.

"I am so sorry, Nova," he said softly. "I've left you

alone in this. I promised you the world, and then I panicked as soon as you got your placement."

His apology felt so out of place, so undeserved. "You're not mad?"

He shook his head. "Of course not. You obviously came to Castor for answers, and I've been so cold to you lately you felt you needed to hide. No wonder you've been unhinged. I practically forced you to be."

I nodded. It was entirely true, but I still felt like a liar somehow. My mind kept tripping on the word 'unhinged.' If what Castor said was true, my somewhat erratic behavior might get worse.

Lan brushed a strand of hair out of my eyes before taking my hands in his. "I promise you that we're in this together. I have a plan to keep you out of the Underworld. One that ends with you and me together. Are you still with me?"

"Yes, of course!" I said, wrapping my arms around him.

He held me tightly, my chest filling with butterflies as I felt like I could breathe for the first time since my totem ceremony. A cough lurched from my throat, startling me as I inhaled a bit of smoke from Castor's little accident.

Lan chuckled, "He's an oaf, but I can't thank him enough for being there for you when I wasn't."

I nodded my agreement though, internally, I couldn't have disagreed more. Castor was many things —mischievous, intelligent, seductive—but he most certainly wasn't an oaf. In fact, that trick with the fire, I'd seen it before. I considered sharing this detail with Lan, but I couldn't riddle out a way to do it without admitting to everything that led me to be found practically naked by the lake with Castor. What was Castor's angle this time? Was he trying to ruin my moment with Lan, or did he just like to watch the world burn? The only thing I was certain of was that his little stunt had been intentional.

Lan tapped on my forehead, "What's going on in there?"

I shook Castor out of my head. "I just wanted to know how you plan on keeping me out of the Underworld."

Lan smiled, filling the whole room with light as he kissed my hands. "I'm going to marry you."

My mouth dropped open, my head spinning as I tried to grasp onto something, anything that made sense.

"I know," Lan said, his voice calm and soothing. "It's sudden, but this is the only way. I don't want to lose you." His gaze dropped to the floor, his voice lowering to a whisper. "You leave tomorrow."

I shook my head, my white-hot blood singeing me from the inside. "We... we've barely kissed. We were only friends just days ago."

"I know. But love is just like what we have, only with some... physical acts. Tonight, just after sunset, I'll come to your room and show you how much more there is for us, and afterward, we'll go to the totems and make the vow."

I stared into his beautiful face, his words brushing over my body like sand across a windy shore. He was the sunshine offering me my salvation, offering me the whole world. Maybe the Totems hadn't made a mistake. Maybe they'd always planned to push me and Lan together.

"And since the totem ceremony torched the promise ring I gave you, this will have to do," Lan said as he knelt in front of me. He reached in his pocket and pulled out a delicate bangle. "Nova, will you marry me?"

I practically squealed the word, "Yes!"

Lan closed the engagement bangle around my wrist right before I jumped into his arms, knocking him back onto the bed with a passionate kiss. I pulled Lan tightly to me as my breaths grew ragged, a flood of new sensations tickling my body as Lan started to tug on my nightgown.

He groaned against my lips, "I'd take you right here if the whole damn place didn't smell like smoke."

I silently cursed Castor as Lan sat up, taking a deep breath as I drank in the sight of him in a whole new light. Hot and bothered, hair tossed, cheeks red, and eyes still latent with lust. I liked seeing him this way. I craved the night he promised me. A night to give him everything and turn us from lifelong friends to husband and wife. Castor was wrong about Lan, and he probably was wrong about me too.

I spent half the day looking for something sexy to wear to bed, only to settle on my nightgown just to be safe. I let my imagination run wild with desire late into the night. When my bedroom door opened, I was eager to give myself away, unable to delay my desire for another moment, but it wasn't Lan who walked through my door to claim me. It was Castor.

CASTOR

Nova's eyes widened as I crossed the room to collect her, the disappointment and confusion behind them banishing most of my guilt. I couldn't let her do this. When Philandro first came to me with his plan to marry Nova tonight, I was relieved that he'd finally come around on her, but the more he talked about it, the less sure I was. He was determined to release her from her Totem with the hopes that everything she was becoming would come to an abrupt halt. By the time he'd mentioned her hair and lip color changing back, I knew I had to stop this. Nova wasn't broken. She was growing into her true self, but I knew there was no way I'd be able to convince either of them of that.

"What the hell are you doing here?" Nova asked, climbing from her bed.

I steeled my nerves, committing myself to the lie. "I

know about the wedding, but something has gone terribly wrong. Lan sent me to take you to the Underworld tonight." My gaze moved to the floor and it took significant effort to look at her again and finish the lie. "He said he'll come for you."

Her hand moved to the engagement bangle around her wrist, lancing me with a sharp stab of guilt.

"What happened?"

I shook my head. "There's no time. We have to go now." I hurried to the closet, pulling out a jacket and handing it to her before I held out my hand for her to take.

She stared at it for a heartbeat, considering whether or not to trust me. Adrenaline tore through me as I felt my window closing. Lan could show up any minute. I contemplated grabbing her and dragging her to the Underworld, but this would be a lot easier to pull off if she went willingly.

She took my hand, her faith in me almost enough to compel me to go back on what I was doing to her, ruining her chances with Lan, and imprisoning her in the Underworld. I don't normally second-guess my choices, but this was different. I wanted to believe I was doing this for the good of Nova, but I wasn't one hundred percent sure. The thought of her sleeping with Lan made me feel already in Hell, not to mention trying to wrap my mind around her marrying him. It wasn't that I wanted her myself per se. The star-eyed girl who'd always swooned over my brother had never interested me, but something in her was changing, and I craved more of it.

I led her to the window and opened it, the muscle memory kicking in from my teen years spent sneaking out to meet beautiful women by moonlight. The window opened, and a gust of cold air whipped into Nova's bedroom. She squeezed her jacket closed as I stepped down off the windowsill onto the soft dirt at the base of the lush forest. I turned to reach back for Nova, and she took my hand, leaping into my arms without hesitation. I let her down gently, and together we moved quickly and silently through the forest, our heaving breaths only interrupted by the sounds of snapped branches as we forced our way through.

We reached the cliff, the frigid air cooling my sweat as I turned to face Nova. She stared back toward the palace, toward her home, toward everything I'd stolen from her. My own heart begged me to have pity and turn back.

I stepped to the cliff's edge, and Nova followed, her red hair glossed with the silver moonlight that also revealed a streaked sheen against her cheek. She took a deep breath, a white plume blooming in front of her before being swept away by the wind.

"Thank you for saving me."

If there was ever a moment to be a good person, this was it, but at the edge of the garden with no prying eyes, I could see the fierceness in her that Lan wanted to snuff out. *Or maybe I'm just a monster who doesn't want to be alone in the Underworld.* The glimmer of her bangle in the moonlight was a whispered response from the Totems that it was the latter, but I didn't care. Lan would most likely give up on breaking her Totem before he'd get anywhere close to the Underworld.

"I'm sorry this happened to you," I said, my sincerity crumbling beneath the weight of my lies.

Since the moment her Totem ceremony began, our fates had been entwined, and despite my not-so-resolute efforts, I'd failed to keep my distance from her. *By the Sol, let me be right about this.* She looked down over the edge, not with the fear of falling, but as if she wanted to see how close she was to saying goodbye to everything she knew. I wanted desperately to offer her a bit of comfort, but I didn't know what the Underworld had in store for us.

"I promise, no matter what comes next, I'll be there."

She nodded somberly.

"Ready?" I turned my back to the edge, my heels hanging over the empty air as I looked into Nova's moonlit gaze. "Your way." I wrapped my arms around her waist.

Her hands slipped around the back of my neck, and I felt her tremble, but I didn't know if it was from fear or cold. I didn't want to risk being seen, nor did I want to lose my nerve, so before I could change my mind, I leaned back, pulling her with me into a total free fall.

PHILANDRO

I could hear howling from outside Nova's chamber, but I thought nothing of it, not until I pushed open the door to find the wind whipping the curtains in front of the empty bed. I didn't pause to consider why; instead, I bounded out through the window to the forest, following a trail of snapped branches and rushed footprints. The cold air chilled me right to the bone as I panted, desperate for answers as a plume of hot breath spread in front of me. I ran clear of the edge of the forest where the footprints stopped and scanned the empty cliffs just as a cloud passed across the moon.

She's gone.

I couldn't shake the image of Nova jumping from the cliffs, but I knew even after what she'd gone through, she'd never let herself fall to her death, especially tonight when we were supposed to say our vows.

Perhaps she went for a little night flight on her dragon and lost track of time, but the knot at the pit of my stomach said otherwise. I returned to the palace defeated, wiping the sweat from my brow as I headed straight for Castor's chamber to tell him the news. If anyone had insight into what was going on with Nova, it was him. I knocked hard on his door, my anxiety growing as the seconds began to add up without an answer. I knocked again but didn't delay before I pushed open the door and stormed inside.

The room was vacant. Suddenly every memory I had of Castor and Nova together was fresh in my mind's eye. *He wouldn't have...* Nova would have told him about our plans. I knew my brother. He wouldn't have gone to the Underworld without saying goodbye, and he certainly wouldn't have taken Nova against her will, which only left me with more questions than answers.

I barreled into my parents' bed-chamber.

Their faces were latent with concern as they sat up in bed.

"What is it, Philandro? You look out of sorts." Mother leaned forward, examining my expression.

I fought to keep my voice steady. "I can't find Castor."

My father's posture relaxed. "Not to worry. He

went Underworld a day early to get his bearings. I'm surprised he didn't mention it to you."

"I'm going after them."

"Them?" my father asked, but I was already out the door.

"Philandro!" My father called, halting me.

I turned back, feeling the distance between Nova and me growing with each fleeting moment. "What is it, Father?"

"It's time that you take your own training as seriously."

I supposed I had been more than a little distracted during our sessions lately. I had sensed my father's growing frustration, but I only needed tonight to get things in order. "Yes, Father. First thing tomorrow morning, I'll be ready to give you my full attention."

He nodded his approval, and I wasted no time before heading out for the cliffs. My focus was locked on getting to the Underworld quickly, and I barely processed the cold weather before I'd climbed onto Fang's back and reigned him off the edge of the island.

I could feel my world unraveling. Ever since father had decided to pass the throne to me, my head had been foggy, filled with thoughts of marriage and the responsibility for the Gardeners, not to mention the world below. I hadn't even noticed Castor struggling with his new burden until it finally came out. I'd tried to be there for him. I was the one he'd come to when the Totems had left him with sparse instructions. I'd made sure he was clear on how to get into the Underworld. I'd even praised him for helping Nova with her placement. Why then, would he go a day early, and what had he said to Nova to make her go with him?

Now I was following the instructions I'd given him, flying east toward the earth and not stopping until I found the forest that looked like a scar on the earth. My determination waned as a second hour passed with no sign of it. My eyes grew weary from searching, the dead of the night starting to whisper doubts into my head. Then, just as I was contemplating turning back, I saw a sliver of blackened, leafless trees at the center of a lush forest. It stood out as described, but had I not been searching for it, I might've passed over without giving it a second look. I guided Fang toward it. My adrenaline surged as we dropped below the tree line and into the shadowy woodland. The branches grabbed at us like barbed hands, and Fang twitched as he searched for an open area to land. The ground appeared to move as we approached, the ash-covered land taking to the air as

Fang's body pushed air through the maze of trees. I eased him down, branches snapping all the way as we landed hard between two spiked stumps.

I slipped off of Fang's back. "Stay here," I whispered as I ventured further through the moonlit wood.

The fog and ash made the trees look like figures, closing in on me as I searched for the altar the text described, but I didn't have to search for long. I came to a small clearing where two trees arched together, their branches woven together to create an empty ring between them.

Swallowing my unease, I ran to it. Caution forced me to wave my hand over it. The gate didn't stir, so I pulled myself through, only to find myself standing stupidly on the other side.

"Brother!" I called out. "I don't know if you can hear me, but if you can, open the gate!"

The wind howled, kicking more ash into the air as I listened for a voice. I knew it was crazy. I knew I was standing in an empty forest talking to myself, but desperation had taken hold.

Castor's voice came from everywhere at once, as if he'd spoken directly into my head. "I can't open that gate."

"You can't, or you won't?" I asked, trying my best

not to let all of my questions flow out at once. His next words struck my riotous fury dead in its tracks.

"We're trapped."

NOVA

I tightened my grip around Castor's hand as the darkness bled into my other senses. I'd never witnessed an equal level of silence or emptiness. Of all the scenarios I'd imagined for the Underworld, an empty black void was the worst among them. It had been a gamble to follow Castor, and I should have waited for Lan to tell me himself that our plans were destroyed. As my shaking legs tried to find footing, my only option was to cling to Castor and search for comfort in the warmth of his hand.

"I want to go back," I said, backing into what felt like a jagged wall where a gateway was a moment ago. Panic rang through me as I peered into nothingness.

"I don't know how to open it again."

My response rose involuntarily. "Open it, Castor! Let me out!"

I could hardly swallow the sound of my own fear

as it echoed back. Castor's grip tightened around my hand.

"Take a breath." He lifted my hands, warming them between his. He breathed against them, his calm tone easing my fear. "We are going to figure this out." He dropped my hands, light emanating from his palm as flames engulfed it.

His face lit with an orange glow, but the light didn't reach far enough to reveal anything except him.

"There's nothing here."

"Don't panic. We don't know that for sure. If anything, I think this is a good sign."

"I suppose an empty, lifeless void is better than hellfire," I mused halfheartedly, my eyes starting to water as I suppressed the urge to cry.

"Exactly. Have you forgotten what the best-case scenario was?"

"The beautiful place from your book?" I asked, swiping at a stubborn tear.

He gave me a sympathetic smile. "Exactly. There was some kind of power source. Look around. Wouldn't you say this needs to be activated somehow?"

"'Somehow' is not as reassuring as you think it is, Cas."

"Good thing it's not my job to reassure you. In fact, I'm technically your king now, so I'll expect you to refer to me as your majesty, your highness, or almighty well-endowed. Your choice."

My mind conjured plenty of nicknames for him, all of which suited him better than the ones he requested. He didn't wait for me to choose one before turning back to the task at hand. He held his arm out, using it to light the way as he ventured deeper into the Underworld.

His silence spoke volumes about his unspoken fears. I, too, listened for movement in the darkness, the scrape of claws on stone, the slurp of demonic blood-lust. I focused on keeping my balance on the uneven terrain, taking each step one at a time.

Castor's flames snuffed out.

"What's wrong?" I whispered.

"Up ahead, I see something," he said, stopping short.

I blinked at the nothingness. "What is it? Are we in danger?"

"No. It's a light."

I reached out to his voice, grabbing his shoulder only to realize he was blocking my view of whatever lay ahead. I peered around him, and sure enough, nestled a few hundred feet in front of us, I saw a faint, blue glow.

I followed Castor as he made his way to it, the dull

light filling me with hope. *Maybe this is the way out.* Castor stopped short, and I ran into his arm as he held it out in front of me. He drew his sword, and the scrape of the sword against his sheath as he drew it filled me with dread.

"Who goes there?" He called. "Show yourself."

A shadow passed in front of the light, and I broke into a cold sweat.

"A thousand pardons, your highness," a voice hissed. "I was not hiding. I just didn't want to frighten you."

I squeezed Castor's arm so tightly that I feared I'd draw blood.

"Let go," he spat.

It took work to obey, but my fingers loosened in time for Castor's arm to light and reveal the small strange creature that blinked at us from a few feet away. His skin was gray in color, his ears were long and pointed, and his two oversized eyes reflected Castor's flames. His stout little body was no taller than my waist, and his hands were occupied with a large dark object that he appeared to be struggling to carry.

"Are you a demon?" Castor asked.

"A Squire, sir. That's the name our kind prefers."

"Are there others?"

"Just me. There's not enough power to sustain more."

He lowered the object to the ground. "Your highness. I mean you no harm. My kind is meant to serve and assist you, but I must admit your weapon is making me feel a bit tense."

When Castor didn't put his sword away, I stepped forward. "Forgive him. He has trust issues. I'm Nova. What may I call you?"

"By the Sol, our very first Nymph. I did not think I'd live to see the day." He walked forward and held his tiny hand out. "I'm Mal'nazur."

I reached for his hand and shook it. The searing white-hot pain scorched my hand, and I ripped it away as a screech tore out of me. Castor's blade was at the squire's throat instantly.

"A thousand pardons. I did not know her powers had not emerged yet."

I rubbed my palm, the coldness of my other hand easing some of the sting. "I'm fine, Cas. Put the sword away."

"I'm so sorry," the squire muttered as he cowered from Castor's blade.

Castor glared at me but relented, once again sheathing his blade, before he leaned close to the small stranger. "If you so much as hurt Nova's *feelings,* it will be the last thing you do."

"Understood, your highness. I-If you will permit me, I would very much like to show you both around. There are some areas to be aware of until her powers come in."

Castor straightened suddenly, his head turning back the way we came. "I have to take care of something... alone."

The folded skin on Mal'nazur's forehead rose, "Just one for the tour then?"

"I'll catch up," Cas said, already heading back.

I turned to the squire for answers, feeling a little more at ease without the risk of Castor stabbing our new coworker of sorts. "Do you know what that was all about, Mal..." I strained to remember the rest of the unusual name, but it escaped me. I took a shot, "...nomo?"

"Just Naz, if it pleases you, miss Nova."

"Naz, got it. Any idea why Castor left like that?"

"It appears we have our first visitor."

CASTOR

Lan's sudden voice in my head was intrusive, my internal dialogue disrupted by his foreign presence. I followed the sound back through the caves to where Nova and I had come through the portal before it vanished, and with each step I took towards it, his voice grew clearer. I'd known he'd come for Nova sooner rather than later, so I had a lie nocked and ready to fire.

"We're trapped," I said in response to his questions.

I was fairly certain it wasn't true, but Lan didn't have to know that, and neither did Nova for the time being. Lying to his face would have been a much harder task, but I couldn't see my brother on the other side of the darkness. Still, I could see his every pained expression in my mind's eye, as if he were standing right in front of me.

"What do you mean you're trapped?" His voice was

wrought with concern that made my stomach churn with guilt. "I'll go to father. I'll ask him to—"

"—Stop."

"But I'm sure he can—"

"—Enough, Philandro. I am King here, and I can sort this out on my own."

He paused, and I feared he could hear my thoughts as his voice danced alongside them in my head.

He sighed. "Brother, swallow your pride. I can get you both out of there."

I couldn't find words that would make him back down, so I let silence fill the air.

The silence hung heavy between us before he responded. "Tell me then. How can I support you?"

His sincerity burned me. He never missed an opportunity to be the better man. "Give me time."

"How much time?"

I was stalling, but to what end? I had to let Nova out of here eventually. Why delay? I'd thought I'd be able to convince her she belonged in the Underworld, but so far, there was little to compel her to stay.

"A year."

"Forget it. I'm going to Father."

His voice was stern, and I reacted quickly. "Ten days."

His silence confirmed my victory, but it felt hollow.

Ten days wasn't going to change a thing, and once Nova and Lan figured out what I'd done, I'd lose their respect. I turned away, heading back down the tunnel toward where I'd left Nova, when my brother's voice rose again, this time almost as a whisper.

"Brother," he asked, "how bad is it down there?"

It was a killing blow to any resentment I'd built up against him since the ceremony. Resentment I still needed to justify my actions.

"It's bearable," I muttered. "I have to go."

I was anxious to return to Nova, especially after the squire had burned her. The last thing I wanted was to lose them. My anxiety eased when I spotted them almost exactly where I'd left them. Nova stood beside the glowing stone that had lured us deeper into the Underworld, her face drenched in blue, ghostly light. Her gaze was fixed on me, and she had a devious smile playing at her lips that thrilled me. I was undoubtedly walking into something that amused her. By the time I reached her, she looked like she was going to burst with excitement, but she held her tongue.

"You didn't get very far," I said, eying the squire who had wandered away a few steps to give us space. "Tell me," I said, halting my mind from conjuring further false hope as it twisted my unspoken desires into stories in my head.

She gestured to the stone. "The power source, it's made of human souls."

I stared down at a strange pulse that moved inside the stone as I inspected it closer. It was a chilling thought, but Nova looked almost giddy.

"We have to *reap* them."

I froze, letting what she'd just said sink in, relishing the delightful feeling that she must've arrived at herself just moments before. I kept my attention on the movement at the center of the rock as a myriad of emotions shook me to life. The raw, undistilled power of being passed such a mantel, the endless possibilities of what this dark empty place could become, and if I was honest, the unbearable attraction I had for Nova now that she'd confirmed beyond a shadow of a doubt that she belonged here just as I did, winded me. The thoughts were all-consuming. For years I'd watched her pine over my brother, not daring enough to speak her heart, not strong enough to command a passing glance or even thought. I'd never seen the fire in her. I'd never paused to wonder why she threw herself off the island day after day, nor why it irked my brother so.

Now, when faced with a task that might've sounded brutal to everyone else in the Garden, the place she'd been cast out of, she showed nothing but genuine excitement. This was only the beginning. I shivered at the thought. There was so much I wanted to show her, and there was nothing more delicious than imagining how she might react to each one. But she wasn't mine. She'd never be mine even if I did buy myself ten precious days. There were lines I could not cross. She might someday come to love the Under-world, but she'd never love me.

Her cold fingers brushing against my forearm jerked me from my thoughts.

"Are you okay?"

I tore my arm away. "I'm fine."

She shoved my shoulder. "Look who's freaking out now."

"I'm not freaking out... I'm just tired."

A shadow shifted in the dark. "Shall I show you to your quarters?" the squire asked.

"Please do."

The small grey figure rolled up onto his toes before he started on his way. "I'll show you to the king's quarters first. Then I'll show miss Nova to—"

"—She'll be staying with me for now."

The squire turned back, his beady eyes fixed on Nova as if he'd expected her to protest, but I knew she didn't want to sleep alone in the dark any more than I wanted her out of my sight.

The squire led us to a set of double doors with a

faint red glow around the frame. "The glowing areas are hot. I'll see you first thing in the morning for your instructions. It'll be nice to finally have some power around here," he muttered under his breath as he disappeared into the shadows.

I pushed the door open, and the first ten feet or so of the hallway glowed a vibrant red, like singed coals. Heat pulsed from it, and Nova rubbed her hands together in front of it. Without asking permission, I lifted Nova, cradling her in my arms and carrying her through the doorframe.

She chuckled.

"What's so funny?"

"It's just tonight was supposed to be my wedding night, and you're carrying me over the threshold."

I wanted to laugh along with her, but every part of that stung. I let her down on the other side, immediately regretting that I hadn't faked a laugh as I'd unintentionally shifted the mood from cheerful to uncomfortable. The chamber felt huge, but it was too dark to see the extent of it. The glowing red accents added a hint of warmth and light, enough to see a bed raised on a pedestal at the back of the room, big enough for ten people.

"Look... Cas..." Nova turned her gaze away from the bed to me.

She's going to say she loves Lan, so I'd better not try anything. She sees me as a friend, or worse, a brother. I couldn't bear to hear any of it.

"Don't make it weird," I interjected before she could say anything that would wound me. "You've already slept in my bed before. Uninvited, I might add. "

She tilted her head, her eyes cutting through me like I was made of glass. I might be moody, but there was no way she could know how I felt about her or that Lan had come to rescue her and I sent him away, but I felt like both of those things were written on my forehead, and I needed to talk to keep her from reading them.

"You're welcome to go find the goblin—"

"—Naz."

"Right, Naz. Have him show you to your quarters if you'd prefer."

Her ruby lips curved into a smile as she took a fist full of my shirt.

She leaned in to speak in a whisper just beyond my lips. "I was promised a wedding night, and I'm going to get one."

My body went stiff. That was not happening, but if she gave it an honest effort, she'd force my hand. I'm not sure I'd be able to say no.

A burst of laughter filled the chamber, the echo carrying further than I would have thought. "I'm totally kidding. You should have seen your face." She shoved me playfully and skipped over to the bed, launching herself on top of it. "This is so comfortable." She groaned. "You have to try this."

She was too innocent to know how badly she was tormenting me. Wasn't she? But then again, since her totem ceremony, she'd undone too many of my buttons for it to be mere coincidence. I only had ten days to find out for sure. Ten days before she'd learn that I'd lied to keep her here. It was too easy to indulge in the fantasy, even if it could only ever exist in my head.

Hell had taken me prisoner, and her name was Nova.

NOVA

I knew where I was when I awoke, but I was less certain of who I was. I could feel the rapid changes inside of me. I could feel the impulses urging me to act on my desires with no regard for consequences. They were powerful. Impossible to ignore. I'd followed the devil to hell, I'd slept in his bed, and I'd even allowed myself to flirt a little. I almost couldn't help it. I craved the way that Castor looked at me when I indulged him, with an intensity that thrilled me. I would never let it go any further than our tumultuous friendship. I was devoted to Lan, but there was a growing part of me that I had to hide when I was with Lan, the same part that seemed to draw Castor in.

"Quiet," Caster groaned, startling me. "You're thinking way too loudly. I'm trying to sleep."

For a moment, I worried he might actually be able

to hear my thoughts. I glared at him, but he was hidden behind a wall of pillows. It seemed he'd had a similar event take place in his head last night.

"Can you really hear my thoughts?"

"You'll never know."

I leaped onto Castor's side, breaking through the pillow barrier and attacking him straight on. He caught my hands, my momentum sweeping me right over him, right off the edge of the bed. I braced myself for impact, but instead of letting me fall, Castor pulled me tight to his body, rolling so he'd land under me at the edge of the platform.

I blinked, stunned by his proximity, my thoughts hyper-focused on his warm body against mine as the smallest touch of amusement flicked the corners of his lips up. Had he always been so seductive? Remembering the very real possibility that he could read my thoughts, I tried to pull myself off him, but his grip only tightened. An intense thrill passed through my body as curiosity urged me not to fight against him again.

"You're going to burn yourself," he said, nodding to the side of the platform, where a thin line of hot embers glowed.

A hint of disappointment churned in my stomach

as Castor lifted me and tossed me playfully back onto the bed.

He sat at its edge. "So, I guess today we're going to reap some souls—get this place powered up."

I shrugged. "We should call for Naz."

Before the name was off my lips, the little gray creature stood at the foot of the bed.

"Good morning, Your Highness and Miss Nova."

"Tell us what we need to know. We're eager to get going," Cas said as I made my way off the bed, carefully avoiding the glowing embers.

Naz moved toward the entrance of the room where the embers burned brightest. "It's quite simple, actually. You walk through the doorway to earth. It will deliver you to a soul that needs reaping."

"How do we know which soul to reap?" Castor asked.

"It will call to you."

A vicious-looking weapon with a curved blade at the top appeared in Naz's hand. The suddenness of its appearance pulled my attention away from the fact that I'd stepped in hot embers and wasn't burned.

"With this," Naz said, "you will touch it to the chest of the human you wish to reap, and you must store the soul until you can input it into one of the Underground's mechanisms."

Cas walked over to me, taking me by the hand. "Are you ready?"

I nodded, feeling a flush of heat as he lifted me to carry me back across the threshold. I should have told him right then that I was no longer at risk of getting burned and I didn't need to be carried, but I didn't, and I had no idea why. *I'll tell him next time.*

He set me down, and I followed him through the darkness of the tunnels. Every few steps, I felt something shift. Heavy boots replaced my thin sandals. Tight leather wrapped my body, and I felt the sudden movement of fabric against the back of my legs as a cape closed around my shoulders. I wasn't sure if Naz was using magic or if the hallway itself was equipping me, but I didn't stop to ask. Naz stopped outside a pair of double doors, handing me a small glass bottle. I stared at it, at the way it seemed to shimmer with anticipation.

"Stick together and call for me when you're ready to return," Naz said.

My gaze moved from the small squire back to Castor, who wore a black-leather suit that fit nicely on his toned body. "Why does Castor get the reaper?"

"Because I am King."

"I don't want to be on bottle duty."

"Too bad," Cas said, turning back to the doors. "We're ready."

With a nod of Naz's head, the double doors swung open, flooding the underworld with the bright white light of morning and the scent of pine trees. We stepped out into a damp forest, taking a wide look around the area as the door vanished behind us.

"Castor." Something familiar gnawed at my stomach. "I think we've been here before."

I looked back to the open square at the edge of the forest as voices carried from within the nearby church.

"I think you're right."

We trudged silently toward the square where a boy sat alone atop a stone wall, staring up at the sky. Castor stepped on a branch, snapping it, and the boy turned around to face us. I'd seen him here before. I could have sworn he'd looked directly at me, but I'd written it off as impossible. Now, as his blue gaze met mine, I knew for sure that this had something to do with my Totem. A totem I hadn't been assigned yet when I'd last been here.

"He's looking right at us," Castor whispered.

"You're back," the boy said casually, his gaze fixed on me.

I stopped in place, my thoughts churning out new possibilities as our task grew more bizarre.

"Do you know me?" I asked, stepping from the forest's edge into the light.

"You were here last week," he said with a grin. "At least I think it was you. Your hair is a different color." He tussled his dusty brown hair, then grinned, as if our bewildered expressions amused him. "It's a small town, and both of you stand out quite a bit. My friends didn't notice you last time, though."

"What's your name?" I asked, feeling a little uncomfortable.

Naz hadn't mentioned anything about hiding from the humans here.

"It's Connor. You guys are angels, right?"

"Not exactly," I muttered.

Cas stepped forward. "You know why we're here then?"

Connor turned his blue eyes to the sun. "Of course."

"And you're fine with it?" Cas asked.

I bit back a laugh. The way things were going, this Connor person seemed like the ageless being, and we the naive humans.

"I've been sick for a long time," he said simply.

Castor's gaze moved to me, and he held out the reaper. "You wanted to do it. Here you go."

I pushed it back with my palm. "I'm not doing it."

"You were all gung-ho for reaping yesterday. What happened?"

I fiddled with the corked lid on the shimmering bottle. "I didn't know the people could see us. This is just awkward."

Connor hopped off the wall, holding his hand out to us. "I'll do it."

"No," Castor said quickly. "You can't do it."

Connor put his hands up defensively. "Just trying to help."

Castor sighed, then lowered the reaper, placing the blade against Connor's chest, but it was my heartbeat that raced wildly. A blue glow lit between the reaper and Conner, and just the sight of the strange light stole my nerve.

"No!" I shouted, snatching the hilt of the reaper, just as Connor's body dropped lifelessly at the edge of the forest.

PHILANDRO

The garden felt deserted with the tributes having gone off to serve their totems, or maybe it was Nova's absence that felt like it filled every inch of the island. Ten days in the Underworld was practically nothing compared to the ten-year sentences the other tributes had to pay. I knew my brother would make sure Nova didn't come to any harm, but I couldn't shake the fear that her time away would change her. I'd always seen her a certain way and these last few days had tested us but brought us closer in the end. But was there a limit? Was it possible for her to drift too far for me to reach?

Before I knew it, I'd made my way to the edge of the island where we often met in the mornings to fly. I stood with my toes hanging over the edge the way she always did, the fearful chill that ran through my body undeterred by my immortality. Before I thought better of it I stepped into the air, my stomach rising to my throat as I raced toward the earth. I only held out a second before signaling Fang. I grasped the air, desperation ringing in my ears until Fang slid beneath me and slowed enough for me to get my bearings. "Home," I said, through clenched teeth as the adrenaline started to sour in my blood. When I was firmly back in the Garden, I lay rooted on the ground, where Fang had dropped me, ignoring the stab of the jagged stones beneath me. I had every intention of going for my morning ride after my little stunt, but my silent fear had reduced me to a puddle. *What was wrong with her?*

I convinced myself that taking on Nova's routine might make me feel closer to her, but now as I lay paralyzed she only felt further away. Who would do that for fun? It was unnatural. I lay still for a long time before I pulled myself off the ground and made my way back home. My father's visit to the Sylph totem was ill-timed. Without his lessons to distract me, idleness was starting to wear on me. My thoughts only seemed to amplify once I broke the outskirts of the forest and into the thicket, where the thick canopy hardly left space for the sun to stream through. There, the whisperings of betrayals and secrets turned to shouts. Then as if an angel came to rescue me from my own damning thoughts, I saw a wisp of Nova's golden hair flash by as a figure moved through the brush. My pulse revved to life, only to strike me motionless when I remembered her hair was no longer that color. It wasn't until I'd almost lost her trail that I realized it was Nova's mother. Curiosity urged me to follow as I made my way deeper into the woods toward the totems.

Before I reached the altar that housed the four totems I heard Nova's mother speak.

"Your Majesty," she said softly.

I pulled back the shrubbery, and sure enough, my mother stood at the base of something I'd never seen before. It was a great dark pillar, similar in size and shape to the other totem poles but much darker in color. My heart sank at the realization that it was the new totem. I wondered why I hadn't thought about there being a new totem pole at the altar, and it probably would have put a damper on Nova and my wedding.

"Good afternoon, Loraine," my mother said, pulling her attention away from the totems.

Nova's mother wrung her hands. "You must know why I'm here?"

"Is it not to pay your respects to the totems?"

Loraine stood very still, looking sheepish like Castor always did when Father reprimanded him.

My mother sighed. "I can't help you."

"Surely, there has to be something you can do. My daughter doesn't belong there."

The corner of the queen's lips turned up. "It's touching to see your concern, especially after you cast her out and she landed in my home." My mother's eyes darkened. "To question the totems is to question the Sol itself. Perhaps there is more to your daughter that you can see. Now, if you'll excuse me," the queen said, turning away and heading back through the woods toward the palace. Loraine stood still long after my mother left, it wasn't until I heard the faintest sniffle that I realized she was crying. Instinctively I stepped through the shrubbery to comfort her.

Her brown eyes widened when she saw me and she wiped away the tears before I reached her. She pointed to the fifth totem, a dark shadow looming over us and said. "That is not my daughter."

"I know," I said softly. I wrestled with telling her everything—about the engagement, about how my shortcomings had landed her in the Underworld. I wasn't sure if she could be trusted, but her similarities to Nova had already worn me down. "I intend to marry her."

Her eyebrows rose. "You and Nova? So the rumors are true. Does that mean she can come home?"

"I'm not sure."

She chewed her bottom lip, waiting for me to continue.

"I went to the Underworld to take her home, but I couldn't get to her. My brother assures me they're alright and that they just need some time to figure out how everything works down there."

"Perhaps I can help? I can take Vex to visit my own totem and see if anyone's heard anything."

I knew it wouldn't hurt to have an extra pair of ears around. If we got lucky, someone might know a way into the Underworld, or a least a bit of lore that might help my brother sort things out.

"Okay. But be careful and discrete, if possible."

Her eyebrow rose.

"My brother is a little sensitive about his new position."

She rested her hand on my forearm and said, "I understand." Before rushing back toward the cliffs.

I took a deep and refreshing breath, as if she'd revitalized my belief that everything would turn out okay. But looking back, I should have known never to ask questions I didn't want the answers to.

NOVA

My mouth dropped open, my gaze traveling from the Connor's body that lay lifeless on the ground to the one grinning beside me. The only difference between Connor before and now, was a subtle glow around his extremities that seemed to get brighter when he moved. Castor's raised eyebrows and frown said he was equally puzzled.

I held up the bottle meant for capturing souls and Connor blinked awkwardly at it. "What am I supposed to do with that?" he asked, taking it. His hand brushed mine, startling me. Was I supposed to be able to feel him? Was he supposed to look like a person? *Something is off.*

"Y-you're supposed to go inside it."

Connor bit back a laugh as he opened the lid on the jam-sized jar and tried to fit his hand inside, only to get stuck with the rim around his knuckles. He looked at me, but I had no more answers than he did.

"This is your fault," Castor spat.

My eyes widened as I turned to him. "*My* fault?"

"Yeah, you stopped me right in the middle, and now he can't fit in the jar."

"Guys?" Connor interjected.

I put my hands on my hips. "Well excuse me if I didn't want him to drop off the wall once we reaped him."

Castor scoffed. "What's it matter if he's already dead?"

"Guys!" Connor shouted, drawing Castor and my attention. "I don't mean to interrupt this love fest, but can we get out of here before someone finds my body?"

We all looked down at the corpse at our feet. "Oh. Yeah, sorry... That might be kind of awkward," I said, my mind conjuring weeping loved ones hunched over our mess.

"Naz, take us back," Castor said over his shoulder.

A portal rushed open beside us, a whirring mass of energy that seeped darkness around us like a smoggy cloud. Castor ushered Connor into it like a prisoner, while Connor cheerfully nodded and took everything in stride like he was on a vacation tour.

Naz stepped back, his eyes wide as he swiped a

hand over his smooth brow. "What have you done?" he asked, glaring at Connor.

"It's Nova's fault," Castor said quickly.

Naz's round eyes moved to me, and I felt a strong urge to explain but all that came out was, "He won't fit in the jar."

"It's no wonder. You botched the reaping. He's completely useless in this form."

"Ouch. I'm sure I'm not *completely* useless."

"A thousand pardons," Naz said quickly. "I only meant, your soul can't be harvested."

Connor's blue eyes glinted. "So I'm only getting pieces but you two seem new to this."

I snorted. "What gave us away?"

"Maybe I can help you?"

"Help us, what?" Castor said, bitterness dripping from his voice.

"Reap souls."

"You want to do that?" I asked, then turned to Naz. "Can he do that?"

"Technically, yes."

Castor ran his hand through his hair. "We don't need help. It would have been fine if genius over here didn't interrupt the reaping. Who even *are* you?"

"Connor," he said flatly. "I thought we've been through this already?"

I pressed my fingertips together. "It's decided then. Connor is going to join us."

"I'm the King. I make the decisions."

"Naz, will you show Connor where he'll be staying?" I asked.

"Yes, Miss Nova. Will you like me to make a room up for you as well?"

I glared at Castor. "Please do."

A flare of heat from Castor's direction caused me and Connor to lean away, but I paid him no mind. Instead, I followed Naz back through the cool damp caves of the Underworld with Connor on my heels.

"The Underworld is quite a unique and vast totem, but it hasn't been tended to in quite some time. I'm sure once you restore it to its former glory, you'll see its charms," Naz said, casually. I tried to imagine what the Underworld might look like all lit up, but it was so dark, that I could barely remember what light was like until I passed back through the portal to the world above.

"This hallway is for Nymphs such as yourselves. You'll find a great many rooms, but I've only diverted our limited power to the first two.

I turned to Connor. "You okay?"

"Never better," he said, offering a smile and heading through the second door.

I made my way into my new bedroom, feeling inexplicably homesick for Castor's room, despite the two being remarkably similar. I sat on the edge of my bed, replaying the events of the day when I heard a sudden rush of water through the walls.

I sat still, listening carefully as I tried to piece together what the sound could be.

"Sunshineeee, yeah. Summer all the time, because you're mine," Connor sang, his voice muffled through our shared wall.

I stood, looking around my apartment for any sign of a shower, but I only saw black stones. I moved to the shared wall on Connor's side and saw a faint glow between the rocks. I ran my finger over it. The wall hissed as the rocks moved. I stepped back, as the dark masses shifted into a sleek kitchen. A bolt of excitement shot through me as I noticed that same subtle glow on almost every surface. I ran to each one, unlocking the secrets of my apartment. Cabinets, closets, a lounge, a window too dark to see out of, a reading nook, some lamps that barely gave any light, and finally a bathroom.

I showered quickly, the warm water thawing my extremities and easing the stress of my day, but I didn't linger. I hurried out of the shower, too afraid of what I'd find if I allowed myself to be alone with my thoughts. I slipped into a nightgown I found in the closet and headed out of the bathroom with my hair wrapped in a towel. I stopped short, suddenly aware that I was no longer alone: strewn on the edge of my bed with a big grin was Connor.

CASTOR

I was more than a little irritated with the botched reaping situation. It was bad enough that Lan thought I was failing miserably in my new position, now we had some guy here who had very strongly implied the same thing. I was starting to doubt whether I was King material or not. Maybe if Nova wasn't so damn distracting. I clenched my jaw at the thought still not warmed to the idea of her moving out of my apartment. At least I wouldn't feel so tempted.

I had to start successfully reaping souls or else this place wouldn't be enough to make her want to stay, but I hadn't expected the process to be as nerve-wracking as it was. I stood completely still in the hallway unable to choose a direction. The last thing I wanted to do was slink back to my empty apartment and think about how badly I was messing everything up. I exhaled through my nose as I made my decision.

"Naz," I called. "I'm going back out, alone this time."

His voice shot out from the darkness beside me. "Very well, Your Majesty. Shall I retrieve your reaper?"

"Please," I said, as I focused my mind on the task ahead.

A portal opened at the end of the hallway, the cold light tainting the warmth of the Underworld as I neared it. Naz slipped the reaper into my hand, the weight of it fueling me as I took the soul jar with my free hand and stepped through.

I didn't realize how nervous I was until I was standing on the cold wet earth alone. What would I do if my unwitting victim begged for their life?

A tree branch snapped and I whirled around to see a member of the Zoi totem, that I recognized from last year's Totem Ceremony. I remembered her enthusiasm after dark before her name. "Robin," I said as it came to me. She approached slowly, her golden eyes wide as she stared back at me. I understood her confusion, seeing another gardener out of context was more than a little jarring, not to mention running into members of another totem while on the job.

"Your Majesty," she said, "what are you doing here?"

"I'm collecting a soul."

Her face lit with understanding and she bobbed her head. "That's right. I heard there's a fifth totem now.

"Are you alone?" she said, a smile playing on her lips as she eyed the empty forest. I bit back a smile. The old me would have gone for that offer in a heartbeat. I could have justified it to myself as a way to bang out my frustrations with Nova and the fact that I could never touch her, but even the thought turned my stomach. I only had ten days to try and power up the Underworld and I didn't want to waste my time on a remedy I knew wouldn't work.

"Like I said, I'm working."

She shook her head. "No matter, I'm sure the other Zoi would love to hear all about your new totem. You must have dinner with us tonight. Bring every one of course. How many might that be?"

"Three and a half."

"Half?"

"You'll see."

Her brow rose. "I'm intrigued. Well I better let you get back to your hard work so you can play hard tonight."

"Mmm."

I turned and headed out of the forest, looking back to see Robin repair a snapped branch before I headed out into a stretch of open farmland with a small house sitting on top. I froze—for a moment it looked like the every hill and mountain was moving, like waves across the land. My footing on the ground wobbled. Dizzy, I blinked my eyes, hoping to steady the world again, and after a few panicked moments, the ground halted beneath my feet. *What just happened?* It was another strange occurrence. Just like when I'd set my curtains on fire and came back a few minutes later to find them in perfect condition. Was this some strange trick of our totem's ability? Or was I just losing my mind?

I looked down at my hand, pulling fire into it and letting it snuff out again and again, wondering all the while what the purpose of it was. There was so much about the Nymph Totem that I didn't know. I didn't know what my abilities were supposed to be used for, but what weighed more heavily on my thoughts was that I also didn't know what good our totem did to serve the world. The other totems seemed to be a bit more straightforward by comparison. I'd have an eternity to search for those answers—for now I had to focus on the soul that called me to the little house.

I tightened my grip on my reaper as I stepped onto the front porch. I knew whoever I'd come for could see me, and in the back of my mind, I knew I should prepare for the very real possibility that someone might try to flee. I opened the door and made my way through the sunlit rooms. The wallpaper was faded, the furniture frayed at the edges, and dust floated through the rays of sunshine that fell through the windows and onto the creaking floors. Finally, I walked into a kitchen where an old woman sat at the table sipping a cup of tea.

"Rolland? Is that you?"

I swallowed a mouthful of unease, deciding on a direct approach. "No, ma'am. I've come to reap your soul."

She grinned a toothless smile. "Oh, Rolland, you look just like your father. Have a seat." She picked up her teapot, absent-mindedly poured tea into a small bowl filled with sugar cubes, and held it out for me.

I was oddly charmed by her. I lay my reaper against the counter and set the jar down beside it, before I took the sugar dish and a seat across from her.

"It's so nice of you to visit," she said.

"I'm only here to reap your soul," I said softly. Forgetting myself I sipped from my cup, instantly regretting the mouthful of sugar.

"So," the woman said. "Is there a special someone?"

"Not really."

"There must be someone. You're so handsome."

I sighed. "Well, I could tell you, but then I'd have

to reap your soul."

"I knew it. Tell me everything," she said, before gleefully sipping her tea. She stopped, staring down at her empty cup before pouring herself another cup. "Can you pass the sugar?"

I grinned and reached across the table, pouring my tea and sugar mixture into her cup.

"Thank you dear." She sipped loudly. "The girl."

"Ah, yeah, well. She's supposed to marry someone else. Actually, she's supposed to marry my brother."

She nodded. "Do you love her?"

"What does that matter?"

She took a deep breath and stared out the window. "Well, if it's a passing fancy it wouldn't be worth hurting the parties involved, but if you loved her, you'd better speak up now, because if you don't, you'll still wind up tied to this person forever, and you'll never be able to escape your feelings for her." She tapped her finger on the table. "So, do you?"

I clenched my jaw, forcefully stopping myself from answering. I set down my cup, and then stood to retrieve my reaper. I knelt in front of her. "I'll tell you, but then I have to reap your soul. Do we have a deal?"

She smiled dreamily.

I leaned in, holding the reaper inches from her chest as I whispered., "I love her."

NOVA

Connor grinned at me from the edge of my bed. "What, you expected me to just hang out all by myself in my room?"

"I felt that same way when I arrived here last night," I said, taking a seat in a chair tucked away in the adjacent reading nook.

He rolled over to get a better view of me. "You can relax. I come in peace."

The sound of his voice reminded me of his singing. My hand lit with sunshine and a gasp slipped out. "Tell me you're seeing this."

"How are you doing that?" Connor said, blocking his eyes.

"I'm not."

"Turn it off!"

The light blinked out.

Connor grinned. "What else can you do?"

I shrugged. "I didn't even know I could do that."

"Can you make it rain, too?"

A thunderclap shook my bedroom as water poured from the ceiling. "Crap!" I screamed.

In an instant, everything was set right, we were dry, and there was no sign that I'd made it rain at all.

"What is it?" Connor asked. "An underworld ability?" He open and shut his hands. "I can't do it."

I shook my head. "I'm not sure. It feels like it, though. Maybe we're supposed to use it to reap souls somehow."

"Well, you and Castor both could use all the help you can get," he said, tracing his fingers over his chest where we'd reaped him.

"Can I ask you something?" I asked, surprising myself.

He sat up. "Shoot."

"You seem to be handling this whole thing remarkably well."

He sighed. "Not a question," he said, softly. For the first time since I'd met him, I saw traces of sadness locked away in his blue eyes. "Well, as I said, I've been dying for a long while, pretty much since I was born. I spent a lot of time speculating about the afterlife and I suppose I'm enjoying having my questions answered. I'm going to miss some people and I'm sure once everything sinks in, I'll have to sort through my feelings on it, but for now, I'm just relieved not to be in pain anymore."

His response was far rawer than I'd anticipated.

"Sorry. I know that's not..."

"No, that answered my question quite well," I said. "Thank you for sharing all that."

He picked at his fingernails. "It's only fair for you to answer one of my questions, then."

I wasn't sure I could match his candor, but I felt I owed it to him to try.

"Why aren't you staying with Castor?"

"What do you mean?"

"In his room. It's obvious you're a couple."

"What? No, we're not a couple. He doesn't think of me that way, and I... I'm engaged to his brother."

Connor clapped his hands and leaned forward, his eyes sparkling with intrigue. "Scandalous."

"I'm making it sound more interesting than it is. Let me start over. I liked Philandro... since the day we met, if I'm honest."

"Then?" Connor pushed.

"Then nothing. That's it."

"So why are you playing house with Castor? Where's your Philandro now?"

"I was placed here during my Totem ceremony."

He rolled over onto his stomach. "No clue what that is."

"Basically, I have to serve my time here to get back to Lan."

Connor crossed his arms. "I'm sorry, I'm not buying it."

"I'm not selling anything."

"I can't tell if you're lying to me or to yourself."

"I'm not lying. I don't feel anything but frustration with Castor."

He pressed his lips together, as if stifling a smile. "Interesting. What kind of frustration?"

"You know, mad. He brings out something in me, something new and scary and I just feel so... hot. Wait, no. That's not the right word."

Connor shrugged. "Well, you've certainly convinced me. I was way off base."

"Lan can help me be everything I wanted to be in life."

"Wanted."

"Want. I meant want."

"What does Castor help you be?"

I held back my response, but it didn't stop the words from echoing through my head. *"Everything I am."*

We sat in silence as I let my mind stroll through

darkened alleys I hadn't allowed myself to before. Connor was way off base. Sure, I'd flirted a little... Castor was just the flirty type. I knew he wasn't serious. He'd certainly never be interested in just one girl, and if he was, it wouldn't be me. My totem placement was a mistake—it had to be, and there was nothing wrong with trying to make the most out of a situation. Lan would come for me, and when he did, I was almost certain I'd be glad about it.

"You're wrong you know," Connor said, out of the blue. "About what you said earlier. Castor *does* see you that way."

My stomach fluttered. "Are you still on that?" There was a small part of me that wanted it to be true, but maybe I was just feeling homesick. He was, after all, the only piece of home I had here.

"Which one do you find more attractive?"

"Why does that matter?" I asked.

"That answers *that* question."

"They're just different. Connor, you need to give this a rest. There's absolutely nothing between me and Castor. You can ask him yourself."

Connor's smile lit up his whole face. "Do you want me to ask him?"

I lifted a pillow and tried to suffocate myself with it. "No..." I yelled into it. I peeled the pillow off my face with every intention of throwing it at Connor but he was no longer on my bed. I heard my apartment door close and I sprung off the couch, heat scorching my body.

"Connor, don't!" I yelled as I bounded down the hall.

"Castorrrr!" Connor called through the darkness.

I turned a corner to see Castor carrying a jar with a bright blue glow gleaming from inside it.

"Connor, don't!"

"There you are, Nova," Castor said, eying mine and Connor's bathrobes warily before shaking the concern off his face. He grinned and held the jar out to me. "Look! I caught us a soul. Where should we put it?"

"Nova wants to know if you're attracted to her," Connor said.

The hallway went silent, the soul in the jar seemed to dim with discomfort as I scrambled for anything to say. But not a single word came out.

Finally, Connor reached out, taking the jar from a frozen Castor. "I'm going to give you two some time. I'll be in my apartment with the music turned up to the max." He winked. "Just in case."

My body burned hot, my gaze glued to the ground even as Connor left with the soul and the light along with him.

Castor turned away. "It's too dark here," he muttered. "Follow me." He marched back toward his apartment.

My heart raced. "Look, Cas, this is all a misunderstanding. Connor is way off base." The door opened to Castor's apartment, the hallway glowing bright red from the embers. He stopped short so I walked past him, eager to get in there and explain myself. "He's just trying to entertain himself by—"

I stopped when I saw the intensity in Castor's dark gaze.

"How long have you been able to walk on the coals?"

"Oh. I, uh... This morning I could—"

"Before I carried you?"

I bit down on my bottom lip. I relished the wild and delicious sensation that surged through me, one that came from being so recklessly honest. Castor's cold gaze struck it dead. This was a massive mistake. What was I thinking? What would *Lan* think? "It's just a crush," I whispered. "It'll pass. I know you don't feel the same way so it's not a big deal." A long silence passed, sucking all the air from the room until I was certain I'd drop right where I stood. "Say something, Cas."

"There's a dinner tonight at the Zoi Totem. We were all invited."

I would have let it go, but something burned inside me, something given to me by the Nymph Totem. The very same sensation that let me walk on coals, made me demand answers. "So you're not going to address my feelings, then?"

"What feelings, you said it would pass. If that's the case it wouldn't be worth it."

"I want to know how you feel about me."

"Why?"

"Look, if you're not brave enough to—"

He closed the gap between us so quickly that my breath hitched. "Don't move," he hissed, through clenched teeth. I obeyed, but it only seemed to make my heart beat harder and faster. With the back of his hand, he traced the line of my face. He slowed when he got to my lips, he ran his thumb across my bottom lip. It was just a gentle touch, but it hurt somehow. His gaze scorched my mouth as I fought the urge to lean forward and kiss him. When had he taken this hold of me? A shiver of excitement tore through my body as he moved down my neck, my chest heaving with labored breaths as his hand brushed over my collarbone. I closed my eyes as he swept over my shoulder and down my arm until I felt a tug on my wrist, that jerked me from my daze. He lifted my arm by my bracelet—the engagement gift Lan had given me—Castor's stare burning me even as his eyes ran ice cold. I caught a rare hint of emotion in them that answered every question I'd asked and many I hadn't.

He dropped the bracelet and my wrist and brushed past me without another word, leaving me to sort through the shattered pieces of the fantasy I almost let destroy my life.

ASTOR

It means nothing. The words were a bucket of ice water over the hope that burned inside me. No matter how many times I thought them, somehow the flames found a way to rage on. She wanted me? When did that happen? If I was honest I couldn't even pinpoint when my interest in her began to shift. *It means nothing.* I paced through the dark rocky tunnels, the nervous energy in my body as excruciating as it was thrilling.

I had to get all of this out of my head and fast. Nova didn't know what I was really like. She didn't know that I'd wrecked her wedding, nor that I'd been holding her captive since we arrived in the Underworld. If she knew, that crush of hers would be extinguished, and she'd most likely never speak to me again. She belonged with my brother. She was going to marry Philandro, who was a better man. But by the

Sol, I'd almost done it. My thoughts got cloudy as she made her little confession and I wanted nothing more than to cross that line with her right there in my apartment. I could have taken full advantage of the situation and given into the delightfully sinful thoughts that had made a permanent residence in my head, but it all fell apart when I saw that damn bracelet.

I was sure my abrupt departure would be enough to obliterate Nova's stirrings for me, and the knowledge that she once felt anything at all for me would be mine to keep and dream about long after I'd lost her.

The scrape of rock in the darkness drew my attention. "Naz?"

"Congratulations on the successful capture of your first soul," he said, lighting a blue flame in the palm of his hand.

I'd already forgotten all about that. "Thank you." I wondered if I should find Connor to get it back or if that was a one way ticket for him to intervene again. I wasn't sure what Nova had told him, but for her sake, I hoped he wasn't egging her on. I wanted her to like the Underworld, that was it. My actions thus far had nothing to do with my feelings for her, and that's exactly how I planned to frame it to Lan when he came for her.

"Have you given any thought into where you'd like to deposit the energy?"

"No, do you have a recommendation?"

"Certainly the kitchen could use it. The apartments are barely functional, especially now that we're powering three. My quarters are a bit—"

"Do you have something pretty?"

His black glossy eyes blinked at me. "Pretty, sire?"

"I want Nova to like it here. Is there something she'd like?"

"Well, of course there are many beautiful amenities, there's a garden, a waterfall, a gemstone cave—"

My cheeks burned hot at the memory of Nova stripping down at the lake's edge. "The waterfall."

"But there are more important—"

"There's nothing more important right now than making this place feel like home. If we can stir up a bit of excitement then we'll be reaping souls left and right."

"I hadn't considered that. Perhaps you're right."

"Shall I go retrieve it from Master Connor, then?"

"No, I'll get it. I should talk to him anyway. Oh, and before I forget, we have a dinner tonight at the Zoi Totem.

"We, sire?"

"You, Connor, Nova, and me."

He stared at me wide eyed and silent, and I couldn't get a read on what I'd said that had offended him. "Of course, you don't have to attend if you'd rather not."

"I would very much like to see the world above. Thank you, Sire," he said, his voice uncharacteristically cracking with emotion.

"Great, I'm going to Connor's. Can I meet you here in ten?"

"Yes, Sire," he said, bowing deeply. I couldn't help but notice the abrupt change in his demeanor, but I didn't have time to inquire further. I turned down the corridor; the dark caves were already starting to feel like home as I made my way toward Connor's apartment.

I stopped outside the door, the soft light around the door flickering as the power strained to keep it lit. I turned back to Nova's room, wondering if she'd made it back. I was tempted to check on her, and maybe clarify that it wasn't that I found her unattractive, I just knew she'd made the right decision when she chose my brother—after all, I was no Philandro. The door to Connor's apartment slid open, startling me from my thoughts. He looked me up and down. "Finished so soon?" he asked with a chuckle.

"I don't hear your music blasting," I said, as I followed him inside.

"You can't blame me for my curiosity." I took a look around the plain and empty apartment feeling a little guilty that he had to stay here. He caught me watching.

"Ah, the apartment is super nice, I just closed everything so the lights would be brighter."

"Closed everything?"

Connor smiled and walked me around his apartment, running his hand over subtle glowing stones to open a slew of rooms and amenities that were hidden away. It took everything in me not to sprint back to my apartment and start touching things.

Connor grinned. "I can't believe you didn't know about this. I wonder what cool things your room has."

"I was just thinking the same thing."

"So what happened with Nova? I'm actually a little surprised she wasn't the one standing outside my door."

I took a deep breath. "I need you not to encourage her. She's just confused. This is a new placement, her abilities and emotions are unlocking. It's not real."

"Are you saying you don't like her?"

"I'm saying my feelings are irrelevant. She's engaged to my brother. Nothing could ever happen between us. He's coming to get her in a matter of days."

He bit back a smile.

"What?"

"You both are a mess."

"Right. Fine. But will you just let it fizzle out? It's better for everyone if you stop fanning the flames."

"Fine, but can I say one thing? I think you're afraid that she'll choose him; that's why you won't admit to liking her."

"I'm not afraid. I have admitted it. Okay? I just can't admit it to *her*."

"Nova's grown. She knows she's engaged, she knows what she'd be giving up. It's her choice to make."

I turned away, heading over to Connor's end table where the soul jar sat. I picked it up, feeling a heaviness in my chest. "She already made it."

NOVA

Naz beamed with pride as he opened the portal to earth, his satin clothing neatly smooth and his demeanor so bright it was almost as if he was someone new entirely. He seemed to be more than a little excited about our dinner at the Zoi Totem by the way he fiddled with his shirt and grinned incessantly, but I had my reservations. For one, I wasn't sure I wanted to face Castor again so soon after being rejected. What had I been thinking? Where did that confession even come from?

Luckily, Castor seemed to be the only one of us with good sense. The more I thought about it, the more I realized that all of my thoughts lately had been of him, and if I was honest, my dreams as well. At first, I thought it was just my mind trying to make the situation bearable, filling my nights with sinful desires I dared not dwell on in the morning, but one push from

Connor had urged me to confront very real feelings. His rejection was the reality check I needed, but in his hesitation, in the way he swept his hand across my cheek, I could no longer deny that at least some part of it was mutual.

But Castor's feelings weren't at fault, mine were. I was the one who'd promised everything to Lan and I alone was betraying him. I had no choice but to forget about Castor and find a way back to The Garden and the life that awaited me there. When I'd returned to my room, I'd expected Connor to pry for details, but he hadn't. I'd taken it as a sign that I'd made the right decision and mindlessly readied myself for dinner. The awkwardness between us had also prevented me from telling him about the little thunderstorm I'd caused in my bedroom when I was chatting with Connor. There never seemed to be a good time to bring it up.

Connor came around the corner, the moonlight from the other side of the portal illuminating his face. "Don't you look nice," he said. "Very assassin-princess." I looked down at my sleek black-fit-and-flare dress, then flashed him my best assassin-princess pose. He laughed, turning his attention to Naz. "And you look very nice as well."

Naz mimicked my pose, our shared laughter easing my nerves until we settled back into the quiet night.

Connor wrapped his arm around me and sighed. "Where is he?"

Before I could think of some witty insult for Castor, the king paced out of the darkness, my stomach fluttering as his gaze swept over me.

"Let's go," he said coldly, before stepping through.

Connor eyed me, the mischief glinting blue at the edges of his irises. "Hangry," he whispered.

It wasn't until we stepped through that it dawned on me that we were about to enter another Totem— one I just as easily could have been placed in. They must've invited us out of curiosity, which was already more generous compared to the frigid reception the other gardeners had shown the Nymph Totem. My stomach twisted. I promised myself that no matter what they said or did, I'd hold my head high.

"Hold on," Castor said, taking my hand and leading me a few paces from Connor and Naz.

My heartbeat stuttered, my hand burning where his skin touched mine. "Look, if this is about earlier, I don't—"

"It's not," he said, the moonlight spilling across his cheekbones.

"Oh."

"You're stressing everyone out."

"I didn't say a word."

"You didn't have to. If this is about earlier, I don't—"

"It's not," I said, quickly.

"Oh. What is it then?"

I shook my head, resenting how easy to read I was. "I'm just nervous about seeing another Totem is all."

Castor looked over his shoulder at Connor and Naz who turned away quickly, as if it wasn't completely obvious they were hanging on our every word. Castor grabbed my wrist and pulled me behind a tree. He pushed me against it, leaning over me with one arm so near my face I could feel the heat coming off of it. My breath hitched, my cheeks flooding with heat that I hoped was hidden under the cloak of night. "The Underworld is your home. Our Totem is as important as any, even if we don't fully understand it yet."

I'd never considered that Castor might have reservations about what we did as a Totem, but his worlds held the promise of someday knowing the truth.

He exhaled slowly and cast at the mossy ground. "Unless you regret it."

"No," I breathed.

"Good. I can't have a Nymph of the Underworld second-guessing her place. Can I?"

I shook my head. I knew full well that he meant my

place in the Underworld, but I was seconds away from blurting 'it's in your bed, my lord.'

"Would you relax?" Castor spat. "It's a party."

"Yes. Sorry. I'm fine. I'll be fine. It's a party."

He rolled his eyes at me as if he had no idea the turmoil he was causing, then turned and trudged back through the thickly wooded forest. Connor whistled as he stepped beside me, nudging me with his shoulder.

"I know," I said, "but I'm letting it go. Tonight will be good for me. I'll see a new totem and remember all the things I used to want."

"Good luck with that," he said.

I turned my smile toward the moon, only this time I noticed that the light peeking through the brush wasn't the moon at all. Tucked away in the trees, high above the ground, was the Zoi Totem.

"There," Naz said, his gray finger extended toward a massive tree up ahead with a thick trunk. As we neared, I saw a girl standing at the base of it holding an oversized tray. Castor, having led the way, reached her first and I hastened closer to hear their interaction.

"I'm thrilled you made it," she said, leaning close to him. I swallowed a fresh mouthful of jealousy. For almost the entirety of the time I spent with Castor, we'd been isolated in the Underworld. I'd almost forgotten how interchangeable women seemed to be to him. Women who knew things I did not. Women with skills I couldn't comprehend. Heat sprung to my hands as the Nymph Totem came to my aid, squashing my doubts and urging me to get in there and compete.

The Zoi girl's gaze met mine, her eyes appraising but not unkind as she offered me a drink before moving to Connor and finally Naz. Castor flashed his teeth as he took a sip, a telltale sign of pain that prompted me to follow suit and taste the liquid from the cup. The liquid was cold but burned hot in my throat and my chest. It rapidly spread to my muscles and eased the tension in my body.

"Welcome," the girl said, "I'm Robin and dinner is beginning upstairs shortly." With a wave of her hand, the tree split revealing a door and a winding staircase that spiraled the inside of the tree. Lanterns flickered like fairies inside. Naz rushed excitedly through the door, clutching his cup with both hands as he followed closely behind Robin, Connor falling in line behind them.

Castor took a long sip from his cup with a wicked smile that threatened to make my knees buckle. It was a good thing I was over him. Good thing I was getting back on the straight and narrow. I was certain, there was no way I would let a little booze make me fall victim to his charms. But I was wrong.

PHILANDRO

Of all the totems, the Atmos' Sanctuary was the only one that competed with the Underworld for most unnerving, mainly because their totem expended a great deal of energy to keep the haven hidden safely beneath the ocean. It was damp and cold, and the Atmos serving there all had features from their extended service that wouldn't fade until they were back in the garden for a significant amount of time. I tried not to stare at the exposed gills or the purple scales, to keep my wits about me as I went about my business. I had invitations to deliver. My coronation was days away and I would have preferred anything to staying put in The Garden and twiddling my thumbs while Nova slipped painfully out of reach.

"Hey stranger," a voice called through the dark. The sound seemed to seep into the restless walls of water as I squinted back through the shifting light. I didn't immediately recognize Rose. Fins and scales aside, she was hardly the giddy teen who fawned all over me just a few weeks ago. Her placement had already changed her. My stomach turned as Nova sprang to mind.

Rose strode confidently toward me, both of her legs covered in shiny purple and blue scales that dropped onto the speckled floor in handfuls, giving way to her pale glossy legs.

"Rose?"

"Who else?" she said with a smirk. She tilted her head as she appraised me, her sleek black hair spilling through the water wall and then falling down at her back. "You look seasick."

"You look—" I shook my head, offering a stunned smile.

She straightened. "Thank you, I'm really enjoying my totem."

"It suits you."

She bit her bottom lip. "What brings you seaside?"

My attention moved to one of the Atmos guys, who swam toward us from the other side of the wall. He banked hard away flashing me a good look at his shimmery tale before he sped past. "I'm actually handing out invitations for my coronation. I thought you might like to attend."

She nodded, pressing her lips together as if she was stifling her words.

"What is it?" I pushed.

"It's just, I'm surprised that Nova is trying to make up so soon. I was a little harsh. Of course, she was overwhelmed with her placement. We all were."

"Actually, I wanted you to come. I haven't really seen much of Nova since she shipped out to the Underworld with my brother."

I wasn't sure why I added that last part.

"That's unfortunate," she said, stretching her arms behind her back, pushing her chest out to tease me. "But she'll be at the coronation, right?"

"Probably."

Her eyes narrowed. "What's going on Lan?"

"What do you mean?"

"You're acting weird. If you have something to say, spit it out."

Lie. "I don't. I'm just not sure she'll want to come back." *Damnit.* It was far too close to the truth for comfort.

Rose's head bobbed back as she let out a full laugh that eased a lot of the fears I'd built up over the last few days, so much so, I almost considered telling her more.

"You think she likes the work in the Underworld? I highly doubt it's the least bit pleasant."

I ran my fingers against the water wall closest to me, trying to observe how much of it wet my fingers, how much dripped to the floor, and how much kept its bizarre shape. "Why is that?"

"Because I hear they're reaping souls."

It was news to me and was more than enough to make me unbearably queasy. I didn't have all the information, but it sounded almost cruel. Rose was right, there was no way Nova would enjoy something like that. I consciously held back my reaction so I wouldn't let *her* know that the Garden had almost no information on the mysterious fifth Totem. "Well, you seem to like your placement just fine. Besides, my brother can be charming if he puts his mind to it." I regretted the words instantly.

"You're jealous," she said with a grin. "Are you insane? Do you know how sexy you are? No offense, but Nova and everyone else that matters has been obsessed with you forever. Your brother has charmed the pants off many of the girls in The Garden, but Nova never even looked twice. I'm telling you, you're insane." She held her hands up in surrender. "And I know I haven't been the biggest Nova fan lately, but I'm coming around."

I nodded; she had made a lot of sense. "Thanks, Rose."

She shook her head with pity. "And as for the job, even if she does like it, she's not going to like it more than Sylph. Do you have invitations to give out there?"

"Yes."

"Why don't you bring her along?" She winked deviously. "Show her what she's missing."

I reached in my satchel and retrieved the invitations. "Would you mind terribly, handing out the rest of these for me? This place is a little creepy."

"You're not staying for the party tonight?"

I shook my head, my face warm as she neared me playfully pouting to convince me, but I was unrelenting. She snatched the invitations and groaned, "Fine."

I tilted my head and drank her in, still processing her brilliant plan. "When did you get so smart?"

"Always, obviously." She shrugged. "But it's hard to notice the genius girl standing next to your crush."

"Hard indeed," I said. I was more than eager to get the hell out of the Atmos Totem, but Rose had renewed my faith in Nova. My brother and I were different and that meant so were Nova and Castor. I knew Nova. I knew what kind of man she needed, and I was it.

And Castor would never fall for someone like

Nova. She was too sweet, too reserved. He'd surely end up with someone bold. As I rose from the depth of the ocean, the platform spraying seawater on my face, I planned our trip to the Sylph Totem. In just a few days, I'd get her back, and this time, I wasn't going to let her go.

NOVA

The Zoi Totem haven was far more beautiful than I could have imagined. The lantern light flickered against the leaves, the treehouse structures lined with fine silks and throw pillows that seemed to marry comfort and elegance with the natural world. The Zoi themselves were a merry bunch, eager to drink and even more so, to urge us to drink and feel welcome.

Unlike Connor and Naz, who were both drinking heavily and letting themselves get lost in the merriment, I held tightly to my cup, only faking a sip when someone posed a toast and insisting I was recently refilled every time someone came by with a refill. I didn't trust myself—not with Castor looking so relaxed and happy. His smile was hypnotizing, and I wasn't the only one caught in his spell. My body stiffened as a flock of Zoi girls fawned all over him, filling his cup until it spilled over, and begging for morsels of information on the mysterious Nymph Totem. I planted myself opposite him at the dinner table, which was less of a choice and more of a battle to the death for his fan girls vying to be in grabbing range. I took a deep breath to steady me, when his dark eyes moved to meet my jealous gaze. My cheeks burned hot as I tried in vain to look away. I only managed to breathe when Castor took a sip of his drink, then answered one of the Zoi girl's questions. I couldn't hear their conversation over the bustle of the festivities, but whatever he said prompted laughter from the girls seated closest to him. Then his gaze moved back to me, his eyes filled with hunger and heat that turned my jealousy to dust.

"Have you tried this?" Connor slurred, as he slopped some green mush onto my plate.

I shook my head, examining the vibrant dishes in front of me.

Naz lifted his napkin and dabbed at his mouth before nodding in agreement. "He's right. You must try that first."

Of all the delicious-looking trays in front of me, the green mush wouldn't have been what I went for first, but I couldn't ignore the rave reviews. I took a bite, recognizing the texture and taste of mashed potatoes instantly, but then whatever the ingredient was that made it green hit my tastebuds with pungent yet quickly fading spice. I devoured the rest and turned my full attention to sampling everything the Zoi had on the table. I was midway through the endeavor when Connor nudged me. I looked up from my plate to find the entire party at a standstill, staring at me. I dropped my fork.

"Will you?" Robin asked, her eyes dim from the ale.

"Will I what?"

"Dance for us. His majesty has so lovingly described your totem ceremony dance, we simply must see it for ourselves."

The memory of that wretched dance sprung forward. The pain, the tears, and the disappointment. I couldn't imagine willingly reliving it. Then Castor stood, grinning as he said, "The moment Nova became mine." He chuckled, "I mean, my subject of course."

A chuckle spread through the crowd, but my gaze was fixed on Castor. Maybe it was the ale, but he exuded joy and pride as he looked at me, as if my Totem Ceremony had always been like a triumph. He reached into his pocket and pulled out the wood-whit-

tled instrument he'd played for me before my placement, his hypnosis already in effect as we walked to the
end of the table. The Zoi, along with Connor and Naz,
crowded around, and I could hear Naz whispering a
more detailed explanation to Connor as we passed,
taking our place at the center of the dance floor. My
heart slammed against my chest as I lowered myself
into my first position, but to my surprise, Castor's
hand came to rest on my waist. With his free hand, he
began to play the same lilting melody on his instrument that kept me awake most nights.

My body moved and Castor along with me as I felt
the heat of him against me. His hand slid down my leg,
then gripped my hip to spin me. The crowd disappeared, and Castor guided me through the dance, my
body obeying every push and pull. He stared down at
me, the whistle of his flute moving me closer to him,
his grip on me tightening as each fluid movement
linked to the next. The movements sharpened as all
that had to remain unspoken spilled out, his greedy
grip on me stealing my breath as my body pleaded for
more. A desperate need built inside, but we raced
toward the end. His hand closed around my wrist. He
spun me to face him, and I bowed deeply into my final
pose, my gaze rising to meet him as the last wavering

note of his flute hung in the air. My pulse raced; my breaths labored as I riddled out how to devour him where he stood. My dance had always been a duet for us.

The erupting applause yanked me from my daze and back to the Zoi Totem. I feigned a smile as the crowd cheered. I turned to Castor who was directing the applause to me, lowering my voice so no one but him could hear me. "You're cruel, you know." I pushed my way through the crowd, smiling wider as the tears threatened to spill. "Thank you," I muttered to the faceless crowd, as strangers hurled compliments at me.

"Wait, Nova," Castor called, but I was determined to get out of there. I pushed my way to the edge of the party, but didn't stop there. I crossed over a rickety bridge to the next platform.

"Stop. Stop." Castor said as he grabbed my arm and turned me back to face him. "Don't play innocent with me. I can't stand it."

I swallowed the urge to slap him.

"You're the cruel one," he said, his eyes darkening as he closed the gap between us. I breathed in the scent of the ale on his breath, desperate to taste it on his lips. Trying to break free of the chemical hold he had me ensnared in and grateful to still have my wits about me.

"No. Believe me, it's you."

"Explain," he hissed through gritted teeth.

I shoved him back, only to move immediately back into his space. "From the moment we crashed to earth that day, you've been tormenting me. Destroying my life with your lies, and your totem, and your fucking suffocating sexiness. I don't have any choice and I can't stand it."

He glared, his eyes falling behind the locks of his dark hair. "Wh—"

"Shut up. I gave you a chance to speak your mind earlier today and you didn't say shit. So now you listen," I said, my voice rising louder than I'd planned. He turned his face away, his keen jawline drawing me in. "You imply that everything is in my head, that you and I are nothing, and then you dance with me like *that*? Do you have any idea how much I want you? It..." I shook my head, trying to find the word, "hurts."

His gaze moved past me, as he released a groan of frustration, before pulling me around a corner into the dark. "You're all talk," he whispered against my lips. The sensation drove me to the edge of insanity, but I no longer had the will to back down.

"Try me," I whispered back.

"Don't. Test. Me. Nova. I will fail." His fist engulfed in flames before he backed away with a long labored breath. He turned away. "You don't know what you're saying. You're just drunk." He took two steps away from me before I found the courage to speak again, but the words stopped him in his tracks.

"Actually, I've been sipping on the same drink all night."

CASTOR

I felt it snap—the last solitary strand of will that had frayed within a whisper of its life to resist her, then it gave out. There was no force on earth or beyond that could stop me as I spun back toward her and dragged her back behind the closest structure to oblige her request. She might have been sober, but the ale had its hold on me, blurring my morality in favor of the white-hot need that screamed for release. My lips met hers, angry and forceful, only to be met with hunger and intensity as we collided. I tasted her tongue, forgetting myself as my hands slipped under her dress, gripping her thighs as she clawed me closer. I waited for her to hesitate, to resist, but as my tongue glided to her neck below her ear, she arched her back and moaned, "More."

I savored her eagerness as she gasped, forcing me to look over my shoulder in a desperate search for anywhere with a modicum of privacy to ravish her. Her body pressed against me, her frenzy taking full control of both of us as I made a quick plan to get her into the building I had her propped against—for her sake, because at the moment, I didn't care if the whole damn party saw what I did to her next.

"Nova!" a voice called.

We froze, my blood running ice cold as I listened for the cursed sound again. *By the Sol, please be my cruel imagination.*

"Nova!" the woman called again.

Nova's eyes went wide. "It's my mother."

A visceral fear tore through me as Nova and I scrambled to be presentable, sobriety slamming into me like a rhino. Nova's mother, hurried across the bridge, squinting in the darkness, her blonde curls tucked into a braid, making her look very much like Nova, prior to her ceremony.

"Mother, what are you doing here?" Nova asked, breathlessly.

Nova's mother's eyes narrowed, her gaze moving to me, as I trained my guilty gaze to the ground. I could only imagine how I looked, hair tossed, lips smudged, clothes ruffled and my fingers still tingling with excitement. The urge to laugh was wicked, so I bit down on my bottom lip to try and stop it. Then her next words were a bucket of ice water on me.

"Lan sent me to find out what's going on with you... Did I... interrupt something?" she asked.

I didn't know how much she knew, but if Lan had sent her there was a good chance she knew that he'd come to retrieve Nova and I'd lied about not being able to leave the Underworld. The fates had spoken: my time was up, and I understood. I was despicable, tricking Nova this way, and now the universe had responded appropriately. I was going to lose her sooner rather than later, and I was fooling myself for thinking any differently.

"No, I was just on my way back to the party," I said, pushing past them.

"Give me a second," Nova said, yanking me out of earshot and view of her mother. She took my hand and laid it against her chest, her heartbeat raging inside. "Feel this?" she whispered.

I nodded. Drinking her in to savor the way she looked at me in these final moments. The brightness of her stare, excitement beaming from those lovely eyes.

"This is for you." She leaned in, kissing me so quickly it stole my breath before she whispered, "tonight," then bounded around the corner back to where her mother was.

Oh, how I wished I could hold her to those words. And, by the Sol, how I envied myself from just minutes ago, even if every part of my brain shouted how deplorable I was for crossing that line.

I gave them enough time to join the party without me, and myself enough time to calm down, physically, before I trudged back to join the others—both the victor and the loser of the greatest prize. The things I would have done to her if we hadn't been interrupted. I had no doubt that I would have gone through with it, probably more than once. And that wasn't nearly the worst of it. I didn't believe in any of that purity crap that Lan lived by, but I was quite certain, I wasn't going to tire of Nova. I wanted nothing more than to keep her, and everything we had was on a ticking clock that she didn't even know about yet.

"Bro, you don't look so good," Connor said, as I plopped down beside him. "Did she yell at you for dry-humping her on the dance floor? Personally, I thought she seemed into it."

"She wasn't," I said, matter of factly, but in my head I was across the bridge on the next platform, still listening to her beg for more as I fingered her. How the hell was I supposed to get that image out of my head? How could I possibly ignore the intensity of her recip-rocation? If I hadn't lied to her, and all of this was for real, I would have had no qualms with taking her—permanently. The hotter the fire inside her burned, the more I craved her, but she didn't know the real me. She didn't know the lies I'd spun to get here and the treasured memories I'd snatched from her ravenous lips couldn't be undone.

"Master," Naz slurred, "I cannot thank you enough for including me in the festivities tonight."

His earnest joy was hard to dismiss, so I said, "As a valued member of our team, you will always be included in Totem-wide events."

His beady eyes grew impossibly large and glassy. "Thank you, sire." He said, bowing his head.

I raised my glass to him in celebration and drank a hearty goblet full.

Across the room, I spotted Nova with her mother, their conversation tense, their expressions austere. I didn't have to hear their words to know what was said, it was all over their faces. Nova's mother did what any loving family member would: she reminded Nova that everything she ever wanted was hers to lose, and that whatever she had going on with me would lead her straight to hell and nowhere else. It wasn't just Lan, the best man I knew, that I was depriving her of, it was her dream totem—the life she wanted for herself.

Despite how desperate I was to keep her, I knew I

didn't have it in me to deprive her of her dream. Later that night, I lay perfectly still in my bed, my chest aching as I forbid myself from taking anything else from her. Nova tapped at my bedroom door, my whispered name on her lips forcing an obstinate tear down my cheek as I lay perfectly still until I could no longer hear her.

NOVA

My mother's words were justifiably harsh as she laid into me. A week ago, a speech that sharp would have reduced me to tears, but I was not the same girl who was humiliated by my placement, nor could I forget that she'd abandoned me in my darkest hour. The combination of those things gave levity to her anger that I doubt she intended. Fortified by my totem, the flames burning inside me incinerated her venom instantaneously, like living armor, my thoughts consumed by the sensation of Castor's kiss as it lingered on my lips.

"And what's going on with you and Castor?" she asked, suddenly drawing my interest. It was a question I very much wanted the answer to as well. A battle to keep myself from looking at him across the table raged inside of me, as my mind replayed that kiss again and again. My body revved back up at the thought of

Castor's body heat against me, the sudden, insatiable hunger that had taken control of me.

"Nova..." my mother pushed.

"N-nothing," I said automatically.

"It better be nothing. Philandro sent me here to find out if you were okay."

Lan's name threw me, skewering me with keen and frigid guilt. Lan had done nothing wrong, nothing to deserve my betrayal. My feelings about him hadn't even changed much. He was still my handsome, dependable friend like he'd always been. What I'd just done with Castor was inexcusable.

I stared down at my hands, trying to imagine the life my mother wanted for me—a life with Lan. It was a beautiful, enviable one with stars and sunshine and companionship. One spent on the back of my dragon, soaring through the damp cold air, but also tightened corsets and royal dinners, and my own quiet surrender as I followed behind Lan with politeness and devotion. I'd secretly imagined it my whole life, only now it was colored differently.

Even after a brief stint in the Underworld away from Lan's stifling morality and the politics of the prying eyes of the garden, I couldn't imagine trying to fit back into the role they'd cast me in. And then there would always be Castor. For all eternity, for every special occasion where the royals congregated, I'd hold my breath to find out if he still held my heart captive. I'd live in fear that my feelings would show on my face, or I'd find myself alone with him and not resist the temptation, or worse of all, one day he'd look at me and I would no longer feel the heat of his desire behind his eyes.

I had more to lose than ever. Castor had this way of seeing me, and the more I embraced who this wanton Totem was turning me into, the more I wanted him. He fanned the flames, he made me unapologetically bold. I didn't care if I looked like an idiot trying to swim in the deep end with someone notorious for drowning the hearts of his admirers. He was worth the risk.

I was certain my mother hadn't intended to solidify my feelings for Castor with her visit, but she had somehow. I had to find a way to tell Lan before I let anything else happen with Castor. It was only fair.

My mom's voice softened as if sensing my remorse out of context. "He's your chance at a better life. Once he's crowned, he can change your Totem."

I nodded, my eyes sweeping across the bountiful vibrant Zoi totem. My desire to be part of the Sylph totem had nothing to do with Lan or Castor and I knew my mother's words rung true, but you don't choose who you are and the Totems don't make mistakes. I was ready to let that dream go and fully embrace the Nymph Totem. I just wished I could have seen the Sylph totem once.

"Why won't you talk to me?" my mother asked.

I looked up. "I don't think you'll like what I have to say."

"Then say something else."

I stood, turning away from the table. "I really appreciate you coming all the way here and trying to make sure I make the right decision."

I glanced over my shoulder to see her eyes narrow in confusion, so I continued, "I don't necessarily believe you know what's best for me anymore, and even if you did, it's extremely difficult to trust you after you turned me away because of my placement."

"Can't you understand how confused I was? It was a lot of new information to take in."

"Yes, I know. I also had hopes and aspirations, and when it all went wrong, I didn't even have my mother to lean on. You know who was there though? Castor."

"It's not too late for you to have the life you wanted. It's not too late to be a Sylph. I know how you looked at Lan all those years, that doesn't just disappear after a few days away. All I'm asking is for you to keep an open mind, and wait to make up your mind until you see Lan again. Can you agree that's fair at least? To him? If after that you still want to get back at me by sullying yourself with that heathen..."

My gaze skipped across the table to Castor, who likely couldn't hear us over the noise, but sat too still to not be paying us some attention.

I leaned in close, lowering my voice as if somehow she'd understand me better that way. "Heathen or not, he and I are one and the same. The sooner you accept what we are and what we're trying to be, the better."

PHILANDRO

My father grinned at me across the breakfast table, his pink cheeks jovial as he ate quietly. My mother, while notably less amused, seemed also to be in good humor in her own quiet way, even though she ate quickly and excused herself to pray at the foot of the Totem Poles as she did most mornings.

"Are you excited for your coronation? You seem downright sunny today."

"Indeed I am, though I lament that Castor didn't get a ceremony as well."

The king bobbed his head. "Yes, well, it was all so sudden and I knew the gardeners would need some time to get used to the idea. If you like, we can honor your brother as well at the event."

I nodded, pleased with the idea and pleased with myself for being such a thoughtful brother. Sweet and sensible Rose, I owed her one. She'd certainly put my mind at ease and given me something concrete to look forward to when Nova returned to me.

After breakfast, I took the long way to the library, drinking in the sunshine and enjoying the splendors of nature before I was once again forced to spend the day pouring over centuries old notes on the four totems. Of course, being so new, Castor's totem had nothing but a title as far as information went, but I hoped to amend that once Castor got the hang of his new post. Perhaps my new bride could fill in the pages on his behalf. I was beginning to think Castor's ten day arrangement would make me a better king for it in the end.

I breezed into the library, taking a seat at my desk and uncharacteristically propping my feet up on the table as I leaned back and thumbed to the details on the Atmos. Perhaps I'd brushed off that totem too quickly. After all, in a matter of days, they'd taken frantic, girlish Rose and turned her into someone formidable.

A shadow darkened my doorway and I nearly toppled out of my chair. I tugged at my shirt to compose myself as Loraine hurried into the room.

"Pardon me your majesty," she said, her brown eyes

startling me with their likeness to Nova's. It was hardly like she'd inherited a single trait from her father.

"Ah, Loraine. Come in, come in." I was all too eager to tell her about my plan, but I gave my best effort to give her a chance to speak first. "What news from the Zoi Totem?"

Loraine's gaze moved to the ground, slapping me with a hefty serving of nerves.

"When I arrived, they were having a celebration to honor the members of the Nymph Totem."

My body went still, my mind reeling. "Were they there?"

She nodded and a long metallic stick fell from her hair, landing with a noisy clang on the floor and spilling her hair over her shoulders. My stomach tightened, she looked so much like Nova with her hair that way that I was tempted to toss the hair accessory out the window, but I remained planted.

"You saw Nova? That's good news, isn't it? It means they got the place up and running sooner than expected."

She wrung her hands. "You need to go down there and get her. Today."

"Is she in danger?"

She shook her head. "No. But—"

"I promised my brother that I'd give him ten days. And I must stand by it."

"You're losing her."

The words were frigid. "What do you mean?"

"You know what I mean."

I turned away, hoping to hide any emotion from slipping onto my face. "I assure you, I don't. And it's no matter, I have a plan to endear her to me once again."

Her eyebrow rose. "Oh?"

"I'm going to take her to the Sylph Totem."

She began to pace. "Interesting. I think it has potential, but it'll take more than her dream to steal her back from Castor."

My voice cracked as my worst fear hung in the air between us. "Steal her from Castor?" I asked, my voice cracking.

Loraine sighed, "She loves you. She always has. But she's an innocent child, and we don't know the lies Castor has been feeding her."

My skin burned hot as I stared down at the floor. "How serious is it?" I asked through gritted teeth.

She shrugged. "A crush, I believe. But that's all it would take for an innocent to be swept up in Castor's depravity."

Her words rang true, and yet, my hesitation was

paralyzing. I'd let my unchecked jealousy corrupt me before. Each time I'd suspected Castor of anything with Nova, I'd been wrong each and every time. But Loraine had planted a seed of doubt, one I couldn't ignore.

"So you're going?"

I nodded. "I think I'll covertly observe their activities today and decide for myself."

"A wise decision indeed. I would expect nothing less from our future King. Will you keep me informed?"

"Of course. Did you want me to give a message to Darren when I visit the Sylph Totem?"

She shook her head. "No, and it's better if you keep Nova out of sight of him while you're there. She's... sensitive about him."

"Understood," I said, but that wasn't the whole truth. Nova never mentioned her father, and the one time I'd asked her about him, she'd shut down the conversation before it began. All I knew were the facts: he'd voluntarily stayed to serve his totem, even after his required service had ended. It happened to be the very same totem Nova had aspired to all of her life. I assumed the two were connected, but I could have easily been wrong about that. It was better to mind Loraine's advice and avoid that minefield altogether.

Without another word I headed out of the library toward the nearest cliff to mount Fang, the nauseating twist of my stomach screaming for me not to go. But the affliction wasn't because I trusted Nova or Castor, it was because I didn't.

CASTOR

Connor grimaced as I handed him the soul jar, its contents swirling around with more vigor than the others we'd collected. Sweat trickled down the back of my neck. I hadn't expected him to run, or be so physically fit when we reaped him. No quiet cups of tea or pleasant conversations in today's reapings, apparently, but that suited me just fine. Keeping busy prevented us from having the conversation I was avoiding with Nova. The last thing I wanted was Connor as an audience to my latest fuck up.

"Are we done?" Nova asked, smoothing some flyaway hairs back into her ponytail.

I'd been waiting for her to call me out all day for kissing her at the party and then leaving her outside my door with no explanation. The fact she hadn't made me suspicious. She was being almost too professional. "Done?"

She smirked at my flummoxed reaction. "For the day?"

"Oh, right. Yeah, let's head back." Time to face the music. But at least it would get me out of the alley and away from the slowly cooling mortal body.

No sooner had the words left my mouth than Naz opened up the gate, greeting us with a smile as we strode through. "It seems you were successful. Well done team. It seems you three are starting to hit your stride."

"Actually, it was a little awkward," Connor said with a laugh, his gaze moving between me and Nova. "Where do you want me to put these?" he asked, holding up the jars of souls.

Naz eyed me for a long moment, a silent conversation passing between us before he said, "I'll take these off your hands."

Nova's gaze caught mine, filling me with the sharp prickles of nerves. I needed out of here before I did something else stupid. Being around her so much was not helping the decision I needed to make.

"I'm calling it an early night. See you all tomorrow," I said quickly, heading for my apartment before anyone could point out that it was barely six. I knew I was a coward, but I didn't know exactly what I was most afraid of. Disappointing Nova, letting her go? Saying the wrong words? Or worse, telling her the truth. The second my head hit my pillow, I heard a knock at my door.

"Sire, you have a guest requesting access," Naz said, his voice both coming through the door and filling my head. "It's Prince Philandro."

I sat up. How many days had it been? Not ten. I still had time.

"Brother," Lan said, his voice ringing clear in my head. "May I speak with you?"

I climbed out of bed and rushed back out of my front door to see Naz waiting for instructions. I nodded and he opened a portal. Not wanting to risk Lan coming through and Nova spotting him, I stepped through quickly, finding myself in the torched forest I hadn't seen since I arrived. It looked different to me now, haunting, beautiful, and full of mystery, just like the Underworld and the girl who had been placed there by her Totem. The portal closed behind me as I stepped closer to my brother. Lan's expression was cold, even with the warmth of the sunlight casting an orange glow on his face.

I clenched my jaw, unsure if I should offer an explanation.

"I'm relieved that you're not trapped in there anymore," he said, as the wind pushed clouds of ash up around our knees.

"We're getting the hang of it."

"You and Nova?"

My gaze dropped from his as my guilt threatened to betray me. "We have others. A squire, and a... I don't really know what Connor is." I forced a laugh, trying to break the tension.

"Nova's mother came to see me."

I had a feeling this was coming, but I had hoped to put it off. "If you have something to say, say it."

He stalked closer with the intensity of a predator, his once sunny eyes glacially filled with anger. "I would ask the same of you."

"I love her."

He stared for a silent moment, as ash danced between us in the wind. "As you love me," he said, his voice cracking. "As I've loved you all these years." He ran a frustrated hand through his hair. "Since we were children, I've looked out for you. Given you everything you ever wanted. Fought on your behalf."

"Yes, I know."

He raised an eyebrow. "Do you? And yet you continue to take everything from me."

I shook my head. "I didn't put her in the Nymph Totem."

"You can't say that for certain. You altered her dance."

"Ask her then. She wants to be here. She might even..."

"What?" he spat.

My thoughts moved to the kiss at the party, and the beat of Nova's heart against my hand. My pulse raced as I said the words, "Love me too."

He smiled incredulously. "You whispered your lies, got in her head, and have the audacity to call it love. If you claim to love me, brother, then you know nothing about the subject."

His mention of my lies weakened my resolve. His gaze bore into me like a hunter locked onto his target.

"Does she even know that I was going to marry her that night? She only knows the lies you've told her. Give her a chance at the life she wants. I can make her a Sylph. I can make her happy."

I took a step backwards. "I didn't plan any of this. It's not some kind of game. I never meant to hurt you."

"Then don't. Take this all back now and I shall never speak of it again. Be the brother I know you are. Kind and quite mischievous. But loyal above all. The brother I know would have died for me and never considered what you're asking of me now." His voice softened. "I beg you, Cas."

I swallowed a lump in my throat, feeling helpless as a child while I listened. It was much easier to villainize him in my head than when he was standing in front of me. For what I'd done, he could have rained hell down on me, and instead was begging me not to hurt him.

He was right. Maybe my lies *were* responsible for Nova's feelings. If she knew the real me, she wouldn't even be here. She would be a Sylph, just like she wanted.

My shoulders folded forward. "What do you want me to do?"

"I'm going to the Sylph Totem to invite them to my coronation. I want Nova to see it. Tell her I'm here, bring her to me, and then..."

I turned away.

"Listen, this last one is the most important."

I looked back over my shoulder.

"Then you let her go."

Unable to move, I stared at the ground in front of me, my body paralyzed by my next task.

Lan's hand landed softly on my shoulder. "You've had your fun. Let's put all of this behind us. She deserves better than this," he said, his eyes sweeping around the charred forest in harsh disapproving judgment. "There are lines even you can't cross, little brother."

The threat in his voice was like a sword at my back, pushing me forward through the portal as if I had no choice at all but to obey.

NOVA

I lay in my bed hours later, my arms crossed over my face as my mind replayed the day. What was Castor's deal? I thought that kiss meant we were finally on the same page, but today was so awkward that Connor didn't even bother coming to rub it in my face. After an entire day of walking on eggshells, I'd had enough. I wasn't sure if Castor had regrets about what happened or if the same guilt that was suffocating me was also suffocating him, but while that kiss had stirred up a lot of questions, it also had answered ones that I'd been asking since I got here.

For starters, I was definitely falling in love with him fast and hard, a fact that had been increasingly difficult to deny and now was too much of a force to ignore. I was less sure *when* it had turned. I wondered if subconsciously I knew it before we'd ever come to the Underworld.

Had I seen something in him the day he helped me with my dance? When we fell asleep together at the palace? When I allowed him to steal me away from my own wedding? Had I known then?

I didn't know the answer to that. But I knew I loved him now.

And how did Castor feel about me? He'd given almost no indication--a heated glance at my bangle, some flirtatious jokes, and then finally a kiss so passionate, it could have melted the sun.

I needed to leave the Underworld, to get back to Lan and tell him how my feelings had changed. When I was sure I couldn't bear to think about it anymore, I leaned on the boldness of my totem and went to find Castor. I reached my front door, pausing for it to slide open.

A stunned Castor stood in my doorway. "Oh," he said. His eyes met mine, searching.

"Cas," I breathed. "I was just looking for you."

"And I you," he said, but his voice sounded off. His shoulders were slouched, his hands twitched, and his smile didn't reach his dark eyes.

"Are you okay?"

His smile widened, but it only looked less genuine. "Yeah, of course." He rolled his neck and he rubbed it awkwardly. "So I wanted to talk to you about that kiss the other night. I mean, I was drunk and we had our fun, but we both know you have to go back to Lan."

It was as if he had set me on fire, the pain instantaneous. My breath caught in my throat. "Cas, I—"

"He's here. Waiting to take you to see the Sylph Totem."

I had to be misunderstanding something. I thought we were finally figuring us out. What had changed? I tried to get him to meet my eyes, without success. "Who's here?"

"Lan. He's waiting for you. Let's go."

My blood boiled hot. "I'm not going anywhere until you talk to me."

"There's nothing to say."

I took slow steps toward him, grabbing him by the shirt and pulling him against me. I put my hand on his chest and felt the wild pulse of his heartbeat against my palm. He stared down at me, his expression pained, the draw between us dizzying.

"I'm in love with you, Cas."

He smiled, the joy radiating from his inner glow, drawing me in closer. He looked down as if hiding from me, his hair fell over his eyes, and I waited, feeling almost like I was back in the middle of the stadium standing by for the King to announce my totem.

Finally, Cas lifted his chin and I saw a tear had left a streak down it.

Fear churned my stomach.

He took a sharp breath in and whispered, "Please, Nova. He's my brother. We...we just can't."

I stepped back, willing my Totem to burn the pain off of my face. I wouldn't give him the satisfaction of knowing how much he'd hurt me. "Okay," I said softly.

"Okay? That's it?"

I nodded. "You were right after all. You don't want me, so there's nothing to say."

"Wait, Nova. It's not that I don't—"

"Naz, I'm ready to go," I said, projecting my voice to be sure I cut off whatever he had to say next. Men were not strong. They were not brave and I couldn't stand there pouring out my heart if Cas couldn't even meet me halfway. I knew how messed up the situation was. I was fully prepared to face the consequences for what I'd done and I had every intention of telling Lan that I belonged in the Nymph Totem.

The portal opened up and I stepped through without looking back.

Lan stood with his dragon outside the gate to the Underworld, just as the sunset made its final show of pinks and purples. He ran to me, pulling me into a big hug that made me nostalgic for my old life.

"Lan, I have to say some things before we go any further."

Using my inner flame, I heated the metal bangle enough for it to bend so I could slip it off my wrist. Then I handed it to him. "I'm sorry, but I can't marry you. And I'm not leaving the Nymph Totem."

He stared down at the bangle for a pensive moment, then grinned brightly, his dimpled cheeks flooding me with memories. "I understand. Feelings change, but can you do me a favor? Will you keep an open mind for a little while?"

"What do you mean?"

"We'll go on a little trip, visit the Sylph Totem for a few days, then we'll go to my coronation. If after the ceremony, you still feel the same way, I'll return you back to the Underworld."

"I'm sorry, Lan, but I don't want to give you false hope."

He shook his head. "It's nothing like that. Just..." He looked down at the bangle, then back at me. "We were friends once, and you said this was your dream. I'll sleep better knowing for certain you made the right choice for you. Won't you?"

I was worried he wasn't talking about the Totems. After all, we didn't choose them. It was strange to have such an offer at all. Didn't the Totems decide? Had they ever chosen wrong before? How long has the king, or future king, in this case, been able to change placement, and if that was the case, why let the Totems choose at all?

My stomach tightened as my thoughts drifted to Castor. He was a liar—since the moment I met him—and still, as he swore there was nothing between us when I was absolutely certain there was, I was all in. We were falling in love, forcefully and mutually, no matter what he said, but I wasn't sure if taking an impromptu trip with Lan would help him sort through his feelings or if it would put a bigger wedge between us.

Lan sighed. "Please, Nova. You owe me this much."

He wasn't wrong about that. I swallowed a mouthful of guilt as I took his hand and climbed onto the back of his dragon. I could never refuse him when he asked so sweetly. "Alright, then. I would like to see the Sylph Totem in person, just once." And with that we took to the sky, the patch of charred forest growing smaller as we rose into the air, straight to the stars.

PHILANDRO

Nova was different. I could see it in her confident gait, the ever-present whisper of mischief in her eyes, but especially in the way she looked at me, almost as if she could read my thoughts. I didn't know exactly what she'd been through in the Underworld but if the murals in our palace were any indication, it must've been truly dreadful. It was no wonder she'd grown attached to Castor. I knew better than anyone just how charming Castor could be when he wanted something. Nova didn't know any better. None of whatever transpired between them mattered, because she was mine again.

The true nature of people didn't change, and as soon as she saw the Sylph Totem in person, she'd know that a life with me was the only one that suited her.

Nova's grip around me tightened, easing my fears as

the sky darkened and Fang raced toward the Sylph Totem, and for the first time since her Totem Ceremony, I felt my optimism return. My coronation, my father's expectations, it all felt more manageable with Nova's arms wrapped around me. The flight was uncomfortably long, so much so that I rarely made the trip, but this was a matter of eternal life. I reflected on the last few weeks, the events leading up to all of this, and I knew it was all so I could take Nova here. A flight that should have dragged for eternity slipped by in the blink of an eye.

Nova gasped as the collection of stars that made up the Sylph Totem came into view. "No way!"

I felt giddy and eager to get off my dragon so I could see her face properly as she drank it all in. The Sylph Totem gleamed in the moonlight. The cluster of translucent pedestals that made the base of the structure were steeped in stardust and silver moonlight. The towering columns framed the area as stars skipped past, drenching the Totem in ribbons of white light. It almost made me wish I was assigned a Totem, like Castor, rather than spending my time in the Garden, watching over my four totems remotely.

I landed Fang as quickly as I could manage and turned to help Nova off, only to be struck completely still.

"What?" she said, barely able to turn her gaze to me, before returning them to the splendor around us.

"Your hair."

She grabbed a handful, staring down at the blonde strands with wide eyes. I wanted to kiss her right there, but I knew if I moved too quickly, I could lose her.

"What does it mean?" she asked as I took her hand and helped her down off of Fang.

"It means you're home."

She smiled shyly, allowing me to lead her to the edge of the totem where we sat and let our legs dangle off the edge. We sat looking out at the Sylphs as they soared through the sea of stars on the backs of their dragons, arranging them as they went.

After a long pause, I said, "So?" and nudged Nova's shoulder with mine.

She took a deep breath. "It's everything I ever imagined." She turned her face to me. "And more."

My chest warmed as I looked at her, shining in the starlight. This was exactly what she needed. And if she could come around about the Sylph Totem, she could about me as well. I was trying to play it cool, but everything was going perfectly. I had no idea her hair color would change, and the implications of it made my head spin. Were the Totems respecting my authority by allowing me to give her the option to become a Sylph or did she always belong here, and just like I'd thought from the beginning, the Underworld had been a mistake?

"Can I ask you something personal?"

She paused and then said, "Only if you can handle an honest answer."

Clearly she thought I was going to ask about Castor, and it stung that she was thinking about him when I was the only one of us who could bring her here. Perhaps she had some guilt she felt she needed to get off her chest, but now wasn't the time.

"Would you be willing to meet up with your father?"

She straightened. "What?" she asked, before shaking the shock off of her face. "I don't know if he would even want to see me."

"He does..." I hoped my extensive planning wasn't going to frighten her off. "He's actually waiting nearby, but just say the word and I'll send him away."

Fear put a sheen of sweat on my forehead as she stood, shaking the stardust off her clothes, her gaze searching the glittering platforms.

"I want to see him."

I stood, taking her hand and leading her across the landing platform, where a figure sat on a glistening bench. Nova's pace slowed when she spotted him. "I'll be right here," I offered.

"Actually, do you mind coming along?"

"Of course, I don't."

She nodded, and I followed her over. As we neared, I could see Nova's father fidgeting, his nerves palpable as we stepped into the dim glow of a columned street lamp. He stood when he saw us approaching. "Nova," he breathed, his voice shaky.

"Dad?"

I had never given much thought to what Nova's father would be like, mostly because she never mentioned him to me, but he had a sort of silent strength even in the midst of such a difficult reunion, that I could respect, the same strength I recognized in Nova.

"You must hate me," he said, his gaze moving to me as if to ask if I was staying for their whole meeting. I certainly was, if that's what Nova wanted. "I should have been there for you and your mother."

Nova tucked a blonde strand of hair behind her ear. "Why weren't you?"

He took a deep breath. "It's difficult to explain. When you have a child, you lose a lot of yourself. I promised myself I wouldn't stay long in my Totem, that it was going to be only last stint in it to get it out of my system, but when I came back here, I got swept up in all of this," he said, raising his arms to a meteor shower of stars overhead. "But, that doesn't mean I don't regret missing you grow up. Now that you're here, maybe we can start over."

Nova stared at the star-studded tiles underfoot, before she looked up. "I'm not saying I would have made the same choice, but I do understand what it's like to fall in love with your Totem. Thank you for answering my questions."

"Nova," he said, but she was already a few paces away. He grimaced at me, a silent plea for help in his eyes that filled me with guilt. I offered an apologetic smile, then hustled after Nova until my pace matched hers.

"That's it?" I asked.

"I don't really know him. I just had a few lingering questions, is all."

"You don't *want* to get to know him?"

She stopped walking and met my gaze with a sweet smile. "What I want is to see every inch of this Totem. Are you up to the task?"

How could I say no? Whatever Nova wanted was what I wanted to give her. "Yeah, I'm your man."

CASTOR

I doubled over to catch my breath, sweat slipping from my forehead and dripping on the jars below. I straightened then pushed the jars toward Connor who was handing them to Naz through the portal.

Connor grinned. "You really are good at this. Maybe you were right about Nova being the problem," he joked but I couldn't even pretend I saw the humor in it. Nova was gone and she wasn't coming back. I'd lied, cheated, and manipulated her to get her here, and it would become clear the second she got some distance.

"Shall I take care of these, Sire?" Naz asked, saving me from whatever cold-hearted response my misplaced anger would have slung at Connor.

"Actually," Connor said, "my apartment could use a bit more power."

Naz's smooth gray face popped through the portal, his beady eyes asking for approval.

I nodded. "Give him as much as he needs, I'm going back out anyway."

Connor's eyes widened. "Wait, no. You can't be serious."

"I'm afraid I have to agree," Naz said. Before I could protest, Naz had magically yanked me and Connor through the portal. I slammed down among the pile of jars.

Frustrated, I stared down at the jars watching the souls move and pulse inside them. It didn't matter how much we powered up the Underworld, it still felt empty and cold without Nova.

I exhaled through my nose. "Take however many you want," I said, my mind blank. "I'll take what's left." Connor stacked soul jars in his arms and Naz carried a few before they headed down the hall, presumably to Connor's apartment.

There were six souls leftover for me to add to the waterfall room. I felt a twinge of joy as I added each one to the chamber, watching a new facet of the room come to life. The first few only brightened the lights. I assumed the rest would do the same, but one made the water itself luminescent, another made plant life bloom from the stones, and the last shifted the rocks to add hidden coves and seating along some of the edges. It was a slice of paradise, and I'd only just begun its renovation.

Nova would have loved this.

The crunch of rock underfoot made me turn to see Connor staring wide-eyed at the waterfall.

"You had a secret swimming pool here the whole time?"

I smiled to myself. "Pretty cool, right?"

"The coolest. Did Nova know about this?"

I clenched my jaw.

He grinned. "Ah, this is for her. I see."

"Was," I corrected.

He walked to the water's edge, where he crouched down, feeling the water with his hand. "You did just add some souls to it. It seems you haven't given up."

"Give it a rest, Connor."

He snorted. "I don't think I will. All you seem to want to do is brood around here. Don't get me wrong, I love the aesthetic, but when it comes time to step up and tell her how you feel, you panic every time."

I didn't want to have this argument. Not with him, not again. It wouldn't change anything, except make me feel worse than I already did. "You don't understand. I lied to her. If I had told her the truth, she'd be married to my brother already."

He cocked his head to the side. "Can I ask you something? What do you like about Nova? Why her?"

I took a deep breath before answering. I didn't like reopening this wound, but Connor had a point about me not giving up, even if I didn't want to admit it. Why was I still pouring souls into this room? "I like that she's fearless, strong, fun, assertive, smart. She knows who she is and what she wants."

"There it is. Smart. Knows who she is and what she wants. And yet somehow you always doubt her. Let me ask you this, had you ever lied to her before you lied to get her here?"

I nodded, feeling a little sheepish but too engrossed in Connor's words to care.

"Did she find out?"

Come to think of it, I'd lied in front of her several times and she chewed me out for it. The memory brought a smile to my face.

"I'll take that smile as a yes. So she knew you were a liar, and yet she took your word for it and ditched her own wedding to come to the Underworld? Sounds like she wanted a way out and you gave it to her."

My thoughts raced, my heart pounding in my chest.

"And then what?" Connor asked. "She confessed her feelings for you, hooked up with you at a party while you continuously rejected her, and then you sent her away, presumably without telling her how you actually feel."

I took off towards the door, then stopped short. He was right. If I could just talk to her, explain, maybe I still had a chance. "I'm—"

"An idiot?"

"Yeah," I said, with a shake of my head. "I think I have to go."

"I think so too," Connor said with a smile. "I'm going to have to start billing you for this."

"And, Connor, uhm..."

"You're welcome, now go get the girl."

I darted through the hallway. "Naz! I need a portal out."

A portal whirred to life and I darted through, landing in the scorched forest.

I whistled for my dragon, my thoughts reeling as I waited for her to descend from the island. Why was I such an idiot? I practically forced her to go with Lan. Nova had been trying to tell me the whole time what she wanted: a placement in the Nymph Totem, and even more surprisingly, she wanted me. She'd told me so again and again, and for some reason, I just couldn't accept that anyone would choose me over my brother. Nova wasn't an idiot. She could make her own choices, and figure out who and what was right for her. Philandro might've loved her first, but what really mattered was who Nova loved.

I'd rejected her and now all I could do was hope I wasn't too late.

The light of the sunset bent around my sky dragon, Nine, as she lowered to the ground, sending a cloud of ash into the air. I was a day late, but Nova would understand. She had to.

I mounted Nine, pushing her to fly as fast as possible toward the Sylph Totem, my stomach in knots the whole way. I had plenty of time to think about what I might say, but nothing felt right.

Finally in the depth of the night, when the sky was darkest and the stars began to shoot around the sky, I reached the Sylph totem.

"Your majesty?" a silver-haired Sylph said as I dismounted.

"I'm looking for my brother, have you seen him?"

She nodded. "He's staying in the guesthouse."

"Thank you," I said, quickly, taking a moment to compose myself. I tried to ignore the splendor of the totem itself. Every bit of twinkling stardust and endless platforms full of delicate structures whispered to me that I wasn't enough, but I stayed the course.

I reached the penthouse of the guesthouse, my

hand stalling before I willed it to knock. A few moments later Philandro pulled the door open. His eyes widened when he saw me, his hair wet, his body wrapped tightly in a robe.

"Brother," he said. But instead of letting me in, he stepped outside, closing the door behind him. "What are you doing here?"

"I need to talk to Nova."

He shook his head. "I can see you're worked up, but I think it's best if you talk to her at my coronation tomorrow. She's asleep right now; we had such an exhausting night. You understand."

I didn't like what he was trying to imply. "Lan," I said, starting my protest.

He cut me off with a sharp gesture. "Go home. We'll see you tomorrow," he said before he slipped back into the room and shut the door in my face as softly as I'd ever seen.

I swallowed a mouthful of jealousy before I decided to poke around back. I whistled for my dragon, trying to stop my head from screaming my worst fears at me. *Stop it.* Lan would say anything to keep Nova. *He's lying.* I mounted my dragon and flew to the back of the guesthouse, staying low to avoid being seen while I tried to get a peek.

My heart stopped when I spotted Nova. She was

alone on the balcony, staring up at the rearranging stars above. She was still dressed in her day clothes, meaning at least some of what Lan had tried to put in my head was all fabricated, but the sight of her filled me with suffocating despair. Long golden strands of her hair cascaded off her shoulders and down her back, her lips a soft pink where they'd been a ruby red. What did it mean? Had she changed her mind so soon? Had she already changed to Sylph Totem? *Fuck. I lost her.*

I banked hard away from the guesthouse, the Sylph Totem, and Nova, and headed directly for the garden. I would attend my brother's coronation tomorrow, and then afterward, one way or another, I'd get answers.

Even if I had to cut them out of my heart, one word at a time.

NOVA

My hair whipped over my shoulder as I leaned over the banister and out to the open air, daring the night sky to swallow me in it. The Sylphs cut through the sky on the backs of their dragons, like flashes of silvery fish under the sea.

The breeze beat against my face, reminding me of my old life, and the same urge to jump I'd always felt whispered to me. Not wanting to worry Lan, I instead opted to whistle for Vex, unsure if he could hear me so far from the garden, nor how long it would take him to travel all the way here if he did. The uncertainty of it made the desire to jump flare, consuming my every thought as I leaned further over the banister.

A sound inside the apartment halted me. I jerked upright, holding my breath to listen more carefully. "She's

here?" a woman said inside the apartment. I didn't immediately recognize the voice and I wasn't sure if I should
stay hidden or go inside Lan's apartment to investigate.

"What are you doing here?" Lan asked, his voice
heavy with irritation.

"A most alarming report has reached me. I must
see her for myself," the woman said firmly as Lan's
reply was lost to the whipping wind.

I stepped closer to the door to try and hear more
clearly. Lan's voice rose, "...intend to marry her and if
you interfere—"

"My visit has nothing to do with your marriage, my
son, no matter how ill-advised your selection. This is
strictly about the totems."

I stumbled back. The queen was *here*. I pulled at
my hair to try to make myself presentable, but the
wind tossed it about. There was a knock at my door
and I hurried back into my bedroom and cracked it
open.

"Nova?" Lan said. "My mother is here and would
like a word with you. Would you mind speaking with
her?"

"Of course not," I said, quickly.

The Queen barely waited until the words were out
of my mouth before she pushed the door open and

brushed past Lan, her multi-layer gown bending around the doorframe.

"Your Majesty," I said, bowing deeply. She nodded toward the balcony so I followed her, checking back over my shoulder to see if I'd at least have Lan for backup. To my annoyance, he remained beyond the threshold of my bedroom.

She strode to the banister and stared out at the stars, not unlike I'd done just a few minutes prior. She took a slow breath and then turned to me so quickly that she startled me. Her gaze was cold, her beauty timeless, and I could see nothing of either of her sons in her features.

I wilted as she reached for me, grabbing a handful of my hair and staring down at it. "When did this happen?" she asked.

"My hair color? It changed as soon as we arrived."

Her brow rose. "When you visited the Zoi totem, did your hair change color?"

How did she know about that? I hadn't given my hair color much thought since I arrived, but now that the queen was here and questioning it, I supposed it could have signified something important. But what? "N-no."

She sighed, turning her attention back to the stars.

"What does it mean?" I asked.

She shook her head. "I don't know. I've spent my life in service and study of the Totems and I've never seen anything of the sort. I was quite irritated that my sons have broken centuries-old rules and brought you to a Totem other than your own. You never should have had any choice at all. That's the beauty of the Totems. Perhaps this means you would have been placed in this Totem had the Nymph Totem not been added this year--and that it comes down to you to decide what kind of life you want to lead."

I nodded. "I see. Can I ask why a new totem was added?"

She shrugged. "You probably know more on that than I do, dear, but everything must either grow or die, and I expect the totems are the same. I imagine you'll be staying in the Sylph Totem," she said, shaking her head. "Then every year anyone placed in the Nymph Totem will be trying to trade. You've made such a mess of things. You're certainly not queen material, despite what my son says in his reports."

Part of me, the Nymph part, bristled at that, even as I had to admit she was right. I couldn't even figure out who held my heart, how would I figure out what the entire Garden needed? "I'm sorry. You're right, I'm not. I never meant for any of this to happen. I was so thrown by my placement," I said. "And Lan tends to exaggerate."

"I was talking about Castor."

My stomach fluttered.

"I actually thought you'd done him some good, what with the way he went on about you and the Underworld. He almost seemed proud of his new position, when he'd been so grim about it before he left."

The thought of Castor writing kindly about me seemed farfetched, but from the moment I was placed in the Nymph Totem and moved into the palace, Castor had seemed interested in the Underworld. Had he just been putting on a brave face for my sake? I bit back a laugh. He was such a liar. Realizing the Queen was still waiting for an answer I asked, "He had? He never told me."

She swept an obstinate hair out of her eyes. "Then I find you here, the Totems giving you an option to choose a new placement and my eldest with the intention of taking your hand."

"I know—"

"And all because you don't know what you want."

"Your majesty," I said, heat tearing through me. A deep crimson red snaked color through my hair before the wind seemed to blow it back blonde with a single gust.

She stared wide-eyed.

"I don't know how *he* feels, but I'm in love with your son."

Her gaze pierced through me, her eyes moving between mine as if reading pages of my diary. As if trying to see which one I meant without asking.

"It took me some time, but I don't need the Totems to tell me who I am anymore."

Her expression softened, her voice low as her gaze moved toward the bedroom door where I'm sure Lan was pretending not to listen. "Then tell me this," she whispered, her voice swept away in the wind. "Do you believe in the Totems Ceremony?"

"With my whole heart."

She nodded, the corners of her mouth tipping up with silent approval. She rested a hand on my shoulder, as her eyes sympathetically wished me luck in everything that came next.

PHILANDRO

The wind stole most of the conversation between Nova and my mother, but the bit I did hear was all I needed to know—Nova had a choice.

No matter how desperately I wanted to hear them, or how close I inched to the door, I wasn't able to hear more of their conversation. I was anxious to see how Nova's mood had been altered by the visit. My mother left as abruptly as she arrived, but I didn't want to rush in and start interrogating Nova. She knew where I was. She'd come out when she was ready.

But after twenty minutes of pining and worry, my willpower snapped. I rushed into Nova's bedroom and out onto the balcony, only to find it empty.

My heart did triple time. My mother wouldn't have... murdered her, right? "Nova!" I shouted. I paced on the balcony, my eyes scanning the stars, my stomach in knots until Vex's iridescent body warped the stars behind him. Nova smirked at me and then dismounted back onto the balcony.

"You scared the hell out of me," I said, my body flooding with relief.

She tossed her hair and reached up to stroke Vex, still facing away from me. "That's a shame, I've been to hell and it's not so bad."

I grinned. "Well, it's nothing compared to all this," I said, gesturing to the sky.

Her shoulders slumped. "We need to talk."

Anxiety pooled at the base of my stomach. "No, we don't. You need to let me show you what I wanted to the night of our wedding." I felt her slipping away, and I only had one card left to play. "I would have married you that night, but Castor lied to you and brought you to the Underworld where I couldn't follow."

She shook her head.

"It's true," I reassured her.

"I love him."

The blade she used was so sharp that the pain barely registered until she said it a second time.

"I'm in love with him." She took a deep breath through her nose then said, "I didn't intend to hurt you. This," she gestured to the stars, "was what I wanted, so much, but it doesn't fit anymore."

I swallowed hard. "Did he say he loved you? He just let you go so easily."

"It doesn't matter."

Anger slipped into my voice. "How does it not matter? You're choosing him and he doesn't even *want* you?"

She crossed her arms across her chest. "I love him."

My face heated. "Will you stop saying that?"

"Then stop acting like you don't hear it!"

I clenched my jaw, anger dulling every other emotion.

"Lan," she breathed, "You don't even want me, not the real me."

How could she say that? I turned away, heading into the bedroom, trying to make my escape before I did something I'd regret. "Don't do that. Don't say shit like that just to make yourself feel better."

She followed me. "I'm serious. We don't fit anymore and if you just took a second to—"

I turned back grabbing her wrist. "Prove it. Kiss me and prove to me that we don't love each other anymore."

Anger blazed in her eyes. She pushed me back onto the bed with a hard shove. Her hair and lips turned a dark crimson, the wallpaper bleeding into a midnight black as her white nightgown burned to a black lace corset.

I froze, my pulse rising as she crawled toward me. Flame sprouted from her hand burning my wrist as a thick metal chain wrapped around my wrist, anchoring itself to the ceiling just as a second chain bound the other.

Heat tore through me, my body's response immediate even as she destroyed my perception of her. Who was this demon? Where was the sweet girl I loved? "Stop," I begged, but the word came out closer to a whimper.

Nova crawled toward me, a devious smile on her face. "How do you want me?" she asked, arching her back and lifting her ass toward me.

"Stop!" I shouted.

In an instant, the room set itself right. Nova sat at the edge of the bed, her white nightgown intact, her blonde hair draped over her shoulder as she stared out to the balcony.

"I don't know what he's done to you... but we can fix it. You don't have to be that. You can choose another path." The words tumbled out. I would be king. I could fix this. Somehow.

She turned her face to me, halting me in place. Streams of tears slipped down her delicate face. "You don't understand. I like being this way. Strong, and confident, and alive. When I'm with you, I feel safe, I stay quiet, I mind my manners and I mount Vex the way I should. But I'm suffocating. Even with all this air up here, I'm suffocating. And I know you meant for me to love the Sylph Totem, and I do, but all I feel is homesickness for my Totem, for my life and even for the guy who broke my heart and sent me away, because he has never looked at me and the wild, sexual, maybe even dirty parts of me with disgust as you just did."

"I'm not disgusted—just surprised," I said, but I wasn't sure.

"Maybe if there was never a Nymph Totem things would be different. I would have been placed in Sylph and our friendship would have bloomed into more and I never would have known about the dark parts of me. And I think we would have been happy. But I know now. I can't *pretend* to fit here with you. I can't play the part of the innocent, silent, flower at your side. I'm not the girl you loved. And I'm sorry for that."

"I understand," I said, wiping her tears. I sat beside her in silence, my gut churning. It hurt, for both of us, but she was right. It wasn't her fault, though. And she had nothing to be sorry for. The blame laid solely on my brother's head.

My mind raced as Nova's words twisted in my

head. Of course Cas never looked at the confident and sexual parts of her in disgust. His appetite was insatiable.

I stood and smoothed my shirt, trying to find the composure years of training with my father had drilled into me. "I invited Castor to my coronation tomorrow. Why don't we just call it a night and I'll hand you off to him there."

"Really? Are you okay?" she asked, sniffling.

"I need some time to think. But yeah, I'll be okay."

It was obvious Castor had corrupted and defiled her and it was up to me to set things right. Tomorrow, once I was king, I'd have the power to do just that.

NOVA

I lay in bed wide awake, staring at my hands, trying to comprehend what I'd done. The walls, my appearance, the chains—they all came from nothing and vanished just as quickly. I had half a mind to hop on Vex and fly back to Castor to pick his mind about it. In the heat of my anger, in my desperation to make Lan understand that I wasn't who he thought I was, or at least who I didn't want to be anymore, I'd done something so inexplicable that I knew sleep was impossible.

As if I needed more reasons to love my totem, it seemed it came with the ability to augment reality, but why? Was it to manipulate resistant souls into resignation? That certainly would beat chasing down the runners. I tried in vain for the next few hours, skipping around my room with my hands outstretched trying to conjure something else, but couldn't manifest even a glimmer of something new. Maybe it was something I could only do when emotions were running high? But wait, I had used it before when Connor came to visit me. I'd made it rain. If I could truly learn to control this ability, it might prove to be extremely useful. It had already gotten me out of a situation that I felt backed into, and it was a shot in the dark to even attempt to use it.

Finally I collapsed back in bed, the relief from my confession to Lan finally settling in. It was a weight I no longer had to carry. Lan would be okay—charming as he was, he'd find the kind of girl he wanted—the kind of girl he thought I was.

But even if Lan met someone tomorrow and married her right away, I didn't know if Cas would ever let himself love me. There was always the possibility that he too could meet someone else, and I'd spend the next ten years in the Underworld drowning in jealousy. But even that life was favorable because I would be fully myself. And nothing made me feel more alive than the utter agony of loving Castor.

I didn't answer when Lan knocked the first time, I didn't want him to know that I hadn't slept. But the day of his coronation promised a lot to do and more to occupy my thoughts as we started rushing about with the preparations.

"Are you ready?" Lan asked, his words tight as he whistled for Fang. Tension dripped off him, and he wouldn't meet my eyes.

I tucked a strand of blond hair behind my ear. "I was actually thinking of heading over on Vex."

His shoulders slouched. "Really?"

"What?"

"I have a lot on my plate today, Nova."

"I know."

"Can't you just," he shook his head and met my gaze, "follow the plan and stop making everything weird? Are we not still friends?"

"We are," I said, but my stomach turned. It seemed like ever since we'd been reunited, he'd been trying to silence me. I'd already been forced into extremes to show him that I wasn't who he thought last night and now it felt like a pattern. I thought it over for a moment, before deciding that it wasn't worth the battle. "For old time's sake."

I hopped on Fang behind Lan and we took to the sky.

The closer we got to The Garden, the more anxious I felt. Something was off. Maybe it was because the last time I was in the garden, my placement was still fresh and no one knew what to make of it. At least back then I had Cas as an ally; now me and Lan

252

were estranged and I was pretty sure Castor hated me for putting him in such an impossible situation with his brother, but that was only the start of it. I wasn't looking forward to seeing Rose, who was angry at the way I'd handled the Totem Ceremony.

Overall, it was obvious that I needed to start making better choices. I made a silent vow to set things right the moment I was given the chance. I just hoped that some of the damage I'd caused could be repaired.

The garden looked smaller somehow when it came into view. It was hard to think I'd spent so much time on it, never feeling restricted by its limits or questioning whether or not I belonged there. Now I couldn't imagine returning to it after ten years. Perhaps there was more of my father in me than I thought.

Fang landed at the edge of the cliffs, and I wondered if Lan had chosen that spot for nostalgia purposes or just out of habit. He grinned at me as he took my hand and helped me down, his honey-colored eyes alight in the sunrise. "I must go prepare for the day," he said, as he kissed my hands.

My face warmed as he looked at me the way he always had. He shook his head, the joy fading from his gaze as he said, "Sorry, I just..." he shrugged, "...missed you." He took a strand of my hair between his fingers and stared down at it before he finally dropped it and started making his way toward the forest. I hadn't thought to check it, but I assumed that once I left the Sylph Totem my hair color would turn back to red. Why hadn't it? What would Castor think if he saw me like this?

I paused, feeling heat burn the side of my face. I looked up toward the forest and sure enough, Castor leaned against a tree, his gaze setting me ablaze as I tried in vain to read his indistinct expression.

My body started moving toward him before I could even protest and we met somewhere in the middle, where the rocky terrain met the start of the grass.

The sudden memory of Castor's rejection slammed into me and I pulled nervously at my hair. "Do you hate it?"

He snickered. "I can tell you've been around my brother, that guy is obsessed with hair color. Personally, I think you look beautiful no matter what color your hair is."

Butterflies fluttered in my stomach, sending waves of heat through me. "I need to talk to you."

"About us? Because if so, I should probably go first."

I paused. "Oh. I... I was actually going to talk about something else, but go ahead."

He rubbed the back of his neck. "Oh. W-what was it that you wanted to talk about?"

The pump of my heartbeat seemed to get louder and louder and I wondered if he could hear it. "I did something strange with my magic yesterday. Something completely new."

"Are you sure it was Nymph Totem magic?"

His question threw me. "What do you mean?"

"Well, you were at the Sylph Totem."

I shook my head. "No, I'm very sure this was Nymph magic."

He nodded, stepping closer. "Tell me every detail."

I paused. Well... this was going to be an odd confession. I frowned, trying to sort out words that didn't sound awful. Somehow, 'I was fake seducing your brother when...' didn't seem like a good start.

"What's wrong?" Castor asked.

"So, last night Lan told me he still has feelings for me."

Castor turned his face toward the forest, his shoulders stiffening. "Ah, okay. Makes sense."

"Anyway, I was trying to tell him that he didn't. I was trying to show him who I really was rather than who he thinks I am, and the sensation came over me that felt like when we light fire, only it was different, pliable somehow." I rubbed a hand over my face.

"This is coming out all wrong. I'm not even making sense."

Castor took a deep breath. "I think that's because you're not telling me everything."

The wind whipped between us blowing my hair across my face. I sighed. "He grabbed my wrists, angry because I couldn't reciprocate his feelings."

Castor's eyes darkened. "He grabbed you?"

"My magic took over. My hair turned red, the walls, the bed, everything changed to the colors of the underworld. My clothes changed too. I manifested chains around his wrists from nothing and I sort of...propositioned him."

Cas stared at me, his silence blaring in my ears as fear sunk into my bones. He took a deep breath. "I think..."

I felt tears prick, the anticipation like a blade at my throat.

"I think I'm going to have to see this for myself," he said with a smile.

I gaped. "You're not mad?"

He sighed. "Mad? No, but I am quite impressed. I think I used Nymph magic to alter reality once or twice, by mistake—I thought I was going crazy." He grinned. "So that's a relief."

I smiled, getting lost in the easiness of his company. I never could tire of it.

"I would have given anything to see the look on his face."

I nodded, letting the relief flush the anxiety out of me.

"I am, however, painfully jealous, so tell me quickly whether he took you up on it because I know he didn't but I can't imagine anyone saying no. No! Wait! Never mind. Don't tell me."

I felt the powerful urge to kiss him, the wind pushing at my back like it was egging me on.

"Nova?" a voice said, from the forest's edge.

I turned to see Rose coming out of the tree line, her gaze moving between me and Castor.

"I should go help Lan get ready," Castor said, turning away and heading into the forest.

Rose approached me slowly, her movements as graceful as her Totem Ceremony dance and her dress every bit as elegant. "You look like you again. Does that mean you actually changed Totems?"

It was nice to see an old friend, even if we'd been at odds. "I'm glad you're here. I wanted to apologize to you for the Totem Ceremony. I should have been more present, instead of worrying only about myself and my placement. I'm sorry."

She smiled, running her fingers along the long blades of grass. "That feels like a lifetime ago. Besides, turns out you had every reason to worry," she said with a smile.

I chuckled.

"Luckily, you have Lan on your side. I hear he intends to marry you. So princess Nova gets everything she wants."

I exhaled through my nose. "I'm not going to marry Lan."

She froze. "You don't have to lie to me, Nova. I'm over him, I promise."

"I'm not lying."

She looked back over her shoulder, pointing back toward the forest with her thumb. "I just spoke to him, he said he's announcing your engagement today at the ceremony."

My thoughts raced, pouring over every detail of my last few conversations with Lan. How could he have possibly misunderstood me? No. There was absolutely no way. I was very clear. He promised me that he'd return me to Cas and my Totem after the ceremony. Rose must've misunderstood.

Uneasiness swelled inside me as I tried to figure out my next move.

Rose tucked a strand of dark glossy hair behind her

ear. "Did I ruin the surprise? He told me so casually, that I figured it was common knowledge. Definitely not a surprise proposal. Please don't tell him I ruined it."

I shook my head. "You didn't ruin anything. I'll handle it." Somehow, I amended.

Just then the music began, corralling guests into their seats for the ceremony. It would have to wait until after his coronation. I would force him to let me go, once and for all, and he could deal with the consequences of his stubbornness after that.

ASTOR

I didn't know why my brother was so incessant about keeping the gardeners away from the palace until after the ceremony. He'd gone on and on about no exceptions, right up until the trumpets sounded and the bells filled the skies with music. The festivities began, with crowds of gardeners arriving on the backs of their dragons from their totems as well as the current garden population all out of their homes and roaming the island at once. There was nowhere to go to be alone and gather my thoughts.

I lamented not taking my opportunity to tell Nova how I felt about her. I'd been so close to spilling my guts but lost my nerve when she started talking about her trip to the Sylph Totem with my brother—not to mention some kind of bedroom activity that I couldn't stop imagining.

I'd practically driven her back into Lan's arms and I just wanted to make sure she knew how I felt before she made her final choice.

Lan looked agitated as my father helped him into his jacket. His hair was messy, his movements jerky, and his usual sunny temperament was replaced with short bursts of anger. I supposed my transition into King had been a little rocky, but I didn't remember coming undone quite as much. Of course, I didn't have nearly as many Totems to oversee, nor the garden to look after, which is why I'd declined to be crowned for my own throne on Philandro's day.

When the time came, I followed my parents out and took a seat beside them on our adjacent thrones, the Centrum overflowing with people all craning for a view of this once-in-a-lifetime event. I scanned the crowd in search of Nova, my stomach roaring with nerves the instant I spotted her.

Her gaze was fixed on me, filling me with enough heat to burn the whole damn garden to the ground. I smiled at her, but she didn't return it, the fire in her gaze singeing me with worry. She lifted her wrist, pointing to it and mouthing something to me, but I couldn't understand. My thoughts flipped back through our time together for clues. I had once scolded her for her engagement bangle which was notably absent, which could mean that in her time away, her feelings hadn't changed and she still didn't intend on marrying Philandro, so why the serious expression?

I shook my head, but before she could attempt again, the music swelled to welcome Philandro as he strode down the aisle from the woods to the middle of the Centrum.

His gaze never moved to me, even as he approached, instead his eyes were fixed on our father's crown. Philandro knelt, in front of our father, the music silencing as our father rose to address the Garden.

"Citizens of the Garden, today I have the immense privilege of crowning my son. As my time as a ruler comes to a close, I find myself immensely proud of the legacy I'll leave in my departure, a legacy that will be carried on by both of my sons."

Our mother nodded, giving me a small smile before turning her attention back on our father. The king lifted the crown off of his head and held it over Lan.

"Do you swear to govern this garden and its inhabitants the way the Totems intended?"

"I do," Lan said, his tone somber beside my father's prideful glow.

"Then I now pronounce you King of the Realm!" our father said, placing the crown on his head.

The centrum erupted into applause as Lan stood to address them. He held up both his hands to quiet the crowd. "Thank you for your faith in me and patience as I try to fill my father's very large shoes."

A warm breeze pushed through the forest and I felt an unexpected sense of peace. It was rather nice to be home for a visit. Lan had taken his place as king as I'd always known he would, and I would run the Underworld, which was certainly not what I'd expected but was turning out to be the best thing that could have happened.

"The Totems have wisdom beyond what we know," Lan said, the crowd listening intently.

The only thing I needed to do now was to confess to Nova how I felt and she hadn't taken her eyes off me since the ceremony started.

"...which is why you deserve the finest. That is why I've chosen Nova to be your queen to rule at my side for all eternity."

His words jerked me from my peace and slammed me back to reality so quickly that for a moment I thought I'd hallucinated the whole thing. Then I realized that Nova had been trying to warn me about this announcement since the ceremony started and I'd been too foolish to see it. A fire raged inside of me, steam engulfing my hands. I had no choice but to flee or risk setting the stadium and everyone in it ablaze, from the raw emotions that had already begun to make my fingertips spark.

I stood and hurried off the stage, sprinting through the forest while I choked on the thinning air. I'd lost her. Just like that. Just like I knew I would and all because I was too much of a Sol-damn coward to tell her how I felt when I still had a chance. I let Lan make me believe I couldn't make her happy, but I could have. I fucking know I could have. I stopped suddenly with the realization that I was standing at the cliff's edge, fighting to breathe as my vision blinked white.

I rubbed my hands over my face too consumed in anger and confusion to think straight or hear the voice calling my name in the distance.

"Castor!" Nova called again, this time ringing in my head like the garden bells.

Heat flared scorching the stones near my feet. "Stay back, I don't want to burn you. Especially now that you're leaving the Nymph Totem."

"Cas," she said, reaching for me. But I couldn't bear to hear her say it, not before I told her everything.

"No!" I yelled stepping back. I felt a rock give out

under my heel and plummet off the edge of the garden. Gravity tempted me, but I resisted. Barely. "It's my turn to speak."

She stopped, her gaze fixed on me, her eyes searching as she watched me unravel.

"I'm madly fucking in love with you and I'm sorry I'm late saying it, but I can guarantee I felt it long before you started admitting your feelings for me. I'm just..." I shook my head. "I'm not as brave as you. I know you've made promises to Lan, but if you pick me, I swear, you won't have to change, you won't have to pretend, you can say exactly how you feel and I'll just love you for it. And this has nothing to do with your placement. The totems could give us a thousand sexy reapers and it wouldn't make a difference. You could go serve your ten years in the Sylph Totem if that's what you want and I'll wait as long as you come back and marry me after." I felt a tear slip out, desperation singing through every word, but I didn't care. "I can make you happy. Don't do this. Don't marry him." The impulse to kiss her was as absolute as death and I reached out for her, knowing that one kiss would tell me everything.

"Brother," Philandro called, his voice halting me. He whistled, and in a flash, Fang swept Nova off of the cliffs in front of me, carrying her toward the setting sun.

I turned to Lan. "What the hell is wro—" His fist collided with my jaw and I slammed down to the jagged rocks on the cliff.

"Stay away from my fiancé," he hissed, looming above me.

I pushed up, trying to get to my feet. "Let her choose."

"She's already chosen. She chose the better man."

I swiped at the sting of my bottom lip, smearing blood onto my hands. "You are not the better man. You haven't been for some time, not since you started believing that the Nymph Totem is less important than the others. You drove Nova away the second she was placed."

"Your lies are the only reason she went with you to the Underworld."

"And what of your lies? Why send Nova away? Is it because you don't want her to have a voice? It's because you don't like what she'd say."

He drew his sword, a weapon that moments ago had been an ornament worn only for his coronation ceremony, now reflected the sunset between us, the sharpened tip at my throat. "I sent her away so she wouldn't have to witness your death. The time for you to corrupt her is at its end."

"You wouldn't hurt me. I know you."

Several faces began to peer out of the forest.

"You know nothing," he spat. "Your immortality will only be broken if you accept my challenge or are you too much of a coward?"

"Son!" My father shouted, from the forest edge. "Stop this at once!"

But Philandro didn't look back. "Sorry, father. I'm the king now."

"I accept your challenge," I said. I was no coward. I promised myself I'd never be that again.

A wicked grin stretched across his face and heat flared into my hand, the flames snaking into a blade. There was no humanity in his eyes—no way I could reason with him. He lunged forward, and I blocked the attack easily, giving me an opening. I didn't take it. I'd caused the pain that drove him here. This could only end with my death.

"Fight back you coward!"

"I can't," I said, blocking his next two slashes. "You're my brother."

I swallowed my fear, tossing my blade to the side as I braced myself for a quick end. He lunged forward, his face filled with fury as his sword came straight for me.

A sudden gust of wind cut through as Vex snaked between us.

Nova dropped in front of Philandro's blade. I tried to move, to pull her aside, but Philandro moved faster.

Shackled by his momentum, the blade tore through her body, spraying me with blood as she collapsed against Philandro's hilt.

NOVA

Philandro stared wide-eyed at me, instinctively yanking his sword out of my stomach and causing me to double over. His bloody sword clanged against the rock as he dropped it, catching me before I hit the ground.

The physical pain was nothing compared to the agony on his face. I struggled to take a breath, feeling the red, sticky blood spread across my gut from the wound. Time slowed, Lan's guttural cry of horror echoing everywhere at once.

"Don't die," he pleaded. "Please Nova, say something."

I studied his face as I coughed once, weakly. The desperation, the grief, all seemed real. "What if..." I wheezed, "my Totem could save me—would you finally let me go?"

His shoulders sank and he nodded. "I would do

anything to save you. Even if that means letting you go for good. I'm so sorry."

Convinced he'd seen enough, I pulled back my magic. My wounds disappeared as I stood and shoved Philandro over with my boot. "Good. Now, I'm going to speak and you're going to listen."

He gaped at me, his gaze moving to my non-existent injury and then back to my face. "You-you tricked me? What kind of sick fucking games are you playing?"

"Welcome to the Nymph Totem. If you think it felt bad killing me, you'd never be able to live with yourself for killing your own brother. I'm nothing to you. You don't even know me, not anymore. I made those promises to you before I knew who I was when I was scared and lost and desperate to hold onto my old life." I smiled at him. "You're going to be okay. You're going to find your queen and she will be everything I am not. You don't love me, Lan. But you do love your brother. He has been by your side since the start and has been tormenting himself for his feelings all this time. Can't you see he'd do anything for your approval?"

I turned back to Castor, who stared so hard at the ground I was surprised the rock didn't spontaneously split in two. His face was neutral but I could see a hint of amusement in his dark eyes.

Lan stood, dusting himself off and shaking his head. "You deserve each other."

"Lan," I breathed. "Your brother needs you to be okay with this."

Silence filled the garden in thick cloudy plumes. Then Lan brushed past me making his way toward Cas. My body tensed, waiting to jump between them again.

Lan reached out, his hand coming to rest on Castor's shoulder. "I'm sorry I tried to kill you."

Castor laughed through tears. "I'm sorry I stole your girl."

"No, you're not," Lan said, a mischievous sparkle in his eyes.

Cas chuckled. "No, I'm not."

Lan's face turned serious. "Don't fuck it up."

Castor nodded.

Lan turned to me. "I need some time. Your ten-year service ought to do it."

"You got it," I said, and when he offered a small smile, I saw the optimistic incorruptible Lan that had been my friend for all those years. He was wounded—lost—but in the tiny gesture, I could see that he'd find his way back eventually.

"Now take your crazy asses back to the Under-world before I change my mind and kill you both."

I took Cas's hand, the heat of it moving up to my wrist, arm, shoulder, up the back of my neck, spreading through my body as my hair turned a dark crimson, my lips tingling with the change.

Cas nodded to Lan and we stepped back over the cliff's edge, plummeting together, recklessly falling, until Vex slithered through to catch us and deliver us to our ashy home. There was a levity to our silence as we flew, an excitement as we moved toward a promising life.

We reached the scorched forest after nightfall, slipping off Vex and sending him off with a thank you before Cas entwined his fingers with mine. A portal whirred open to welcome us, and Naz and Connor stood on the other side to greet us.

"Welcome home, miss Nova," Naz said with a grin.

Connor started to slow clap, his gaze fixed to mine and Cas's interwoven fingers. "It's about damn time."

"Connor, music," Cas said with a smile.

Connor clicked his tongue. "You got it chief," he said as he headed gleefully back to his apartment. Naz smirked as Castor pulled me through the dark hallway. My heartbeat raced with anticipation, but Castor didn't make me wait. The moment we turned the corner, he pinned me against the wall, his lips finding mine.

His kiss made my head spin and in it, I could feel everything he'd been holding back. I held him so tightly my body shook, clawing at his shirt only to find it already burning to shreds.

"We're banished," I said, my smile wide as he tortured me with the sweetest kisses on my neck.

He chucked. "Whatever will we do for the next ten years?"

"I have some ideas," I said, ripping away what was left of his shirt. It felt so good to be free--so right to be home. All I wanted to do was surrender to all of my desires and show Castor that he was everything I wanted. If not for him, I might've spent my whole life jumping from cliffs just to feel like I did every second in the Underworld and every moment beside Cas.

"Wait," he whispered, "come with me." I clenched my jaw in frustration as he pulled away, grabbing my wrist and leading me down the hall. I expected him to pull me towards his apartment but he passed right by. Before I could speculate, he opened a passage, and I knew the sound instantly. *A waterfall.* The room lit, the warmth of the misty falls filling the air as we walked into paradise. It was more than anything he'd promised me that night we stayed up dreaming of everything the Underworld could be.

I stood in awe, trying to resist the powerful urge to cry. "How did you do this?"

He took me by the hand and led me into the water, my body pulsing with desire as he pulled it to his. "Welcome home, my love," he whispered against my lips.

Two hours later I lay exhausted at the edge of the falls, feeling the pulse of Castor's heartbeat against my cheek as he drew circles across my naked body with errant water droplets.

"I can't believe you did all this for me," I said, biting back a smile.

He laughed, "This is really just the beginning. We'll spend an eternity collecting souls and unlocking the secrets of this Totem together. And even sooner, we'll need to make this place presentable for when we host the Gardeners for our wedding."

My heart stopped as I sat up, wide-eyed. "I don't remember you asking me to marry you."

Cas grinned, climbing back into the water before pulling me in and wrapping my legs around him. The warmth of his body made me shiver. "Really? I asked you like twenty minutes ago."

"Liar."

He stole a kiss before shaking his head.

"Well, what did I say?"

"You moaned yes, over and over again."

I felt delirious in my happiness, having finally found my place and my person. Knowing every day might be just like this one. "I don't think that counts," I teased.

"No? All right well," he said, drawing me in for a slow kiss. "Hop on and I'll ask again. And again, as many times as it takes."

"Deal," I said. "I can be a bit of a slow learner, be patient with me?"

"Always, my love."

Try One of My YouTube Audiobooks!

The Fae & The Fallen

A shot at the legendary Fae Academy leads a non-magical girl to confront her sexy nemesis.

Kingdom Cold

A teenage princess attempts to murder her betrothed.

Eleven Wings

A traitor arrives in Purgatory. Can a sexy stranger change her fate? Or is history doomed to repeat itself?

Milton Keynes UK
Ingram Content Group UK Ltd.
UKHW032048180324
439698UK00004B/291

9 798224 737864